BRAIN GAMES
STORIES TO ASTONISH

Third Flatiron Anthologies
Volume 9, Book 29, Fall/Winter 2020

Edited by Juliana Rew
Cover Art by Keely Rew

Brain Games: Stories to Astonish
Third Flatiron Anthologies
Volume 9, Fall/Winter 2020

Published by Third Flatiron Publishing
Juliana Rew, Editor and Publisher

Copyright 2020 Third Flatiron Publishing
ISBN #978-1-7339207-9-7

Discover other titles by Third Flatiron:

(1) Over the Brink: Tales of Environmental Disaster
(2) A High Shrill Thump: War Stories
(3) Origins: Colliding Causalities
(4) Universe Horribilis
(5) Playing with Fire
(6) Lost Worlds, Retraced
(7) Redshifted: Martian Stories
(8) Astronomical Odds
(9) Master Minds
(10) Abbreviated Epics
(11) The Time It Happened
(12) Only Disconnect
(13) Ain't Superstitious
(14) Third Flatiron's Best of 2015
(15) It's Come to Our Attention
(16) Hyperpowers
(17) Keystone Chronicles
(18) Principia Ponderosa
(19) Cat's Breakfast: Kurt Vonnegut Tribute
(20) Strange Beasties
(21) Third Flatiron Best of 2017
(22) Monstrosities
(23) Galileo's Theme Park
(24) Terra! Tara! Terror!
(25) Hidden Histories
(26) Infinite Lives: Short Tales of Longevity
(27) Third Flatiron Best of 2019
(28) Gotta Wear Eclipse Glasses

License Notes

Contents

Grins & Gurgles

*****~~~~~*****

Editor's Note

Life's become something of a shifted chessboard, hasn't it? Welcome to the Fall/Winter 2020 edition of Third Flatiron Anthologies, with the theme, ***Brain Games: Stories to Astonish.*** We particularly sought science fiction and fantasy stories featuring puzzle solving and ingenuity, inverted tv tropes, inventions (clockwork, practical, or Rube Goldberg), masterful creations, and social commentary. A number of these tales cross over to the dark side, in keeping with the season, and our final short story ushers us into the winter holidays.

We open with an odd space mystery, as asteroid miners try different theories about who stole their Earth shuttle. Brian Trent gives us "Theft, Sex, and Space Pirates."

Further bending our minds, Geoff Taylor gives us "Killer dApp," software scifi that presents a completely evil yet plausible way to take advantage of anonymous cryptocurrency (hey, kids, don't try this at home). Jetse de Vries dishes out Japanese AI warrior scifi, with embedded poetry.

With the coronavirus playing havoc with people's smellers, it could be important to keep our noses in tip-top health. Two of our stories disagree on what space aliens smell like. Alyce Campbell is pretty sure they smell garlicky ("Kwatt Games"), while Brenda Kezar speculates that they smell like patchouli ("US Portal Service"). Maureen Bowden dips into "The Sweet Smell of Sheep" to tell the story of the Trojan War from Paris's ex-wife.

As we are encouraged to stay in our homes and socially distance ourselves, mail delivery becomes an even more important daily service, not to mention that postal service is a pillar of civilization. We're not so sure a quantum portal would be a good replacement. Rebecca Fung posits that Santa might agree with us, as he gets all his toy ideas from kids' letters, in "The Greatest Toymaker in the World."

Artificial intelligence, androids, and robots seem to be on a lot of people's minds. That is, do they have minds like us? Henry McFarland describes some "Perfectly Rational Gamblers," and their frequent visits to casinos, while C. J. Peterson writes the code that would determine whether two supercomputers have achieved self awareness (hilarity ensues). But could we be living in a computer simulation? In Paula Hammond's "All Your Bases Yada-Yada," a woman discovers what seems like a glitch in the pixels on the way to work. It's a bittersweet symphony. Although they didn't have 3-IN-ONE oil back in Medea's day, she helps out Jason and the Argonauts against a giant robot that's prone to rust, in Jenny Blackford's "A Bronze Giant to Guard Her."

For you players of games: A cop in training gets too comfortable living in virtual reality in Jess Hyslop's "Softlock."

Intelligence different from our own may arise from Nature, as Ellen Denton reminds us, in "Minds Unseen."

We hope to rely on good old-fashioned human ingenuity to get us out of scrapes like deadly viruses. Let's see what the Nobel Peace Prize address in "Stockholm, 2066" might be, as told by Joseph Sidari. And we wonder what Graham J. Darling is referring to in his comical postapocalyptic tale, "The New Season." Is it the new flu season, or the election season? And which is scarier?

Editor's Note

Lisa Timpf shows us it's possible to do our shopping without all of today's "helper technology," in "The Disconnect."

Halloween season wouldn't be complete without some horror tales. Eleftherios Keramidas's sorcerer just can't resist applying the latest technology to outsmart a deadly magical book, in "Toxic." Monica Joyce Evans's "Forced Teaming" discusses the cons of a job holding the digital copies of dead human personalities. For some Frankensteinian steampunk, Dennis Conrad's "The Incredible Machine" sucks the life out of us. Otherworldly calls come in through a village's outdated switchboard in David Rogers's ghostly "Numbers." In M. Richard Eley's "Bad Connection," a hacker gets his just comeuppance when he Zoom-bombs the wrong meeting.

To spice things up, Justin Short offers "Mock Me Amadeus." (It's a graveyard smash.) Dominick Cancilla recounts the adventures of "Joey and Rue," a riotous mashup of demons and Rube Goldberg, while M. K. Hutchins writes an empathetic tale about getting on the Grim Reaper's good side in "Upcycling Death."

As usual, we conclude with the flash humor section, "Grins and Gurgles." If you're fed up with the constant pillow guy commercials, Steve Zisson tells us how to DIY your own. Aidan Doyle channels his lovable evil villain to lecture his minions in "To All the Creatures I've Hid from Ethics Committees," and Lauren Lang's lingerie model suffers the discomfort of outer space to find "The Best Bra for the Boobs."

Until we dream of life and life becomes a dream (Always),

Juliana Rew
October 2020

*****~~~~~*****

9

Theft, Sex, and Space Pirates

by Brian Trent

"This is unacceptable!" cried Director of Mining Operations Michael Alverson. His shrill voice resonated throughout the asteroid hangar. "I *thought* we were all in the business of improving things! I *thought* we were united in our commitment to making tomorrow better than today! Do you see the problem we're facing?"

The miners gathered in a half-circle, blinking at him without comment. Clearly, they didn't see anything except for the empty hangar.

"It's empty!" he added.

"We can see that, Mike," said Jolene Fort. She stood with her fellow miners, dressed in the bulky white biosuit required for shifts in the ice caverns below. "Why don't you calm down and tell us what—"

"Someone *stole* our only shuttle!" He pointed to the dusty outline on the floor where the mining camp's sole means of off-rock transportation had been securely docked. "We're marooned!"

Jolene crouched to examine the floor, then turned her attention to the mooring clamps. Her gaze strayed next to the hangar doors—they were sealed, of course, although fresh silicate from the surface littered the area around the threshold.

11

Alverson paced, twisting his handkerchief. "Aren't we on the same team? We provide water to space-faring society! We provide raw materials to keep the economy flowing! We share the same goal of improving lives! *And someone here stole our shuttle!*"

"We can radio in for another one," Jolene said. "The company isn't going to leave us stranded here, Mike."

Alverson's eyes fixed on her. "Not the point! We've suffered a theft!" He whirled around, lab coat billowing like a pale cape, and touched the base intercom. "All personnel report in, sector by sector! This is an emergency roll-call!"

It took ten minutes for every sector in the asteroid to comply. Each researcher, miner, engineer, and assistant spoke their name and corporate ID, and the electronic security panel glowed with the accompanying biometric confirmation and present location.

"All accounted for," Jolene muttered, touching the hangar floor with her gloved hands. The tarmac was wet, she noticed. Streaks of clear water made wriggling shapes towards the dusty outline where the shuttle had been.

"Exactly!" Alverson roared. "So there's only *one* explanation!"

The group looked at him expectantly.

"Space pirates! This was the work of space pirates!" And he turned his glower onto Jolene Fort.

Jolene, however, did not return the look. "Check out this water on the floor."

"You're a space pirate!" Alverson repeated.

"Never proved, Mike."

"You robbed the Jovian Spin Tower!"

"Never convicted." She let out a weary sigh. "Come on, I've lived among you folks for months, earning my keep, and never stealing or sabotaging or space pirating anything. Besides, even if I was a pirate, why would I steal a shoddy little rock-runner? *How* would I

12

steal it, since I'm *standing in front of you?* Seriously, check out this water." She glanced to the ceiling. "I don't see any pipes here. No signs of leakage from the surface. So, where did these puddles come from?"

"Space pirates. . . ?" someone suggested.

Alverson snarled, "It obviously came from the lagoon! Where the ice miners work! Where one particular ice miner who *used to be a pirate* was on duty when the bay doors opened and the shuttle flew off!"

The miners looked awkwardly from Alverson to Jolene. The lagoon lay in the asteroid's center, an ever-melting reservoir of ice collected into cisterns for off-rock shipment. It was the lifeblood of their operations; their drinking water, their fuel, and their supply line to the deepworlds.

Jolene steepled her gloved hands and squatted, considering the wet squiggles on the floor. They seemed to lead to the main hatch, which in turn led straight to the lagoon, but they didn't appear to be in the shape of boot-prints. If anything, it seemed like someone had dragged several sopping wet towels or hoses across forty meters of floor to the mooring clamps. Maybe someone had carried several leaking drums to the shuttle and absconded with them. . . .

"Any drums missing?" she asked.

The director checked the inventory sheet on the security panel. "No, they're all on base."

"Any missing equipment? Drills? Filters?"

"No."

"Towels? Hoses?"

He blinked. "No! What kind of questions are those?"

She held out her hands helplessly. "Mike, I'm trying to understand what exactly was stolen."

"The *shuttle* was stolen!" he roared.

"Yes, but it's only a means of transport! We have valuable things here, but the thief ignored all that. Which suggests the thief only wanted to escape from here. Problem is, all employees are accounted for."

"A wily space pirate," he said coldly, "would sabotage us from within. I propose *you* snuck into the hangar, set the shuttle to autopilot, and sent it to a prearranged coordinate for your pirate associates to grab it!"

"I don't have pirate associates."

"You robbed the Jovian—"

"Never convicted. However, I *do* agree with one thing."

The miners stared at her.

Jolene pointed to the wet tarmac. "This *is* lagoon water. That's the only place it could have come from."

Alverson reviewed the security panel, scrolling through the biometric check-ins. "There were fourteen miners on last shift in the lagoon."

"Fourteen miners," she agreed, "and a couple hundred eels."

"Excuse me?"

"We have eels in the lagoon, Mike. Lots and lots of eels."

The group nodded. They knew about the eels, of course. As recently as a year ago, robots had been used to lay fiber-optic cables for asteroid operations throughout the lagoon, to repair filters, to crawl through pipes for fixing leaks and removing sediment blockages. But robots broke down, and replacement parts had to be shipped in, and robot technicians were expensive to maintain. A new solution was needed.

"A year ago," Jolene said, "We shipped in a few hundred genetically enhanced, intelligent eels to replace the robots."

Alverson sneered, "Intelligent? Hardly! They're only a little smarter than rats. Barely sufficient to be trained for our needs."

"Nonetheless, they *are* smart. And when they work together, I've seen them solve problems no single eel could have. They exhibit true swarm intelligence, emergent problem-solving by virtue of their aggregation."

Alverson gaped at her. "Are you actually blaming the theft of our shuttle on. . . on. . . "

Jolene shrugged. "Eels, yeah."

"*Eels?* We have a *known space pirate* in our midst, and she's blaming *eels* for this theft! Eels!"

"Enhanced eels," someone muttered.

Jolene rubbed her chin thoughtfully. "Sargasso eels, right?"

The group stared with renewed interest at the wriggling, squiggling trails on the floor. Finally, Abraham Dennings, head chef of the base's kitchen, raised his hand and said, "You're right, they *are* Sargasso eels. Taste really good fried or barbecued, served over seasoned rice with a dash of lime."

But Alverson squared off to Jolene. "And just how did you know what kind of eels they were? More to the point, *who cares?*"

"I guessed. We got them a year ago. The timing makes sense."

"What timing?"

She paced around in a circle. "I think it's interesting that you're always talking about how we're creating a better future—how we're in the business of making tomorrow an improvement on today—but that's really a matter of perspective, isn't it? Sure, we've kept the economy flowing. But we also kept an intelligent species as our prisoners. As our slave labor force. We trained them, worked them, and then ate them when they were too weak to be of further use. So what kind of positive life did *they* have?"

The director of mining operations made a caustic sound that might have been a laugh. "You have some audacity, Fort! You expect us to believe that every eel on base got together, squirmed their way to the hangar, and hijacked our shuttle for some kind of joy-ride?"

"Depends on how you define 'joy-ride.'"

"And just where do you think they went?"

Jolene comfortably held the older man's gaze. "Earth."

"*What?!*"

"Every year, wherever they are, Sargasso eels return to where they were born: the Sargasso Sea on Earth. Racial memory, instinct. Call it what you will, but it's a known fact of the species. It's what they do, and what they have done for millions of years. They always return to their birthplace, by any means necessary."

Alverson stomped his foot. "But *why*, damn it?"

. . .

The shuttle dropped through Earth's atmosphere like a meteor. It auto-deployed its parachute, splashing down into a thick tangle of seaweed. The impact caused the ocean to surge and heave. Bobbing on the surface, the hatch popped open.

The eels poured out into the sea of their ancestors.

Then, with the frenzy of eons, they began to mate.

About the Author

Third Flatiron welcomes back Brian Trent. More of his work has recently appeared in *The Magazine of Fantasy & Science Fiction* (July/August 2020), *The Year's Best Military and Adventure SF,* and two upcoming anthologies from Baen Books.

*****~~~~*****

The Art of the Duel

by Jetse de Vries

Don't believe all those extended fighting scenes in the blockbuster movies: those are bullshit. Especially the long-drawn duels between the hero and the villain, as true fights to the death between exquisitely trained warriors last seconds, a minute at the most. I know, as I'm facing Kaeyen right now, and one of us will be no more, very soon.

Kaeyen's naginata strikes at me—its shiny pole's reflection causing quick, distracting flashes—as I parry, parry, and parry. It seems like I'm on the defense, but there are feints within feints within feints. I'm looking—actively inviting—that single crack in her armor, that singular opening in her movements. Then I will follow through, fast as lightning, without mercy, deadly.

As that is the true art of the duel: find that single opportunity that exposes your opponent, and finish her off. Any true warrior will not waste time and effort on theatrics. And Kaeyen needs to go.

She wants to become the next Protectress of Oshi no Kyo—the Zen master of neural networks—but that will only happen over my dead body. He's mine, and I am the only one who truly understands his art. For I am an artist myself, a warrior-poet, my poetic skills merged seamlessly with my samurai kills. And Oshi no Kyo is a warrior, too, albeit in a different realm. Therefore, we are soulmates, and that bitch Kaeyen will not have him.

I fight for life using my
skill to prepare and to die
earn his love and to do
what it takes to strike through

There it is—between her expert moves, her flashy strikes, her striking flair—the minuscule yet morbid window of opportunity. The lapse of attitude creating the gap of latitude. I move in to finish her.

But what is this? She uses my pre-emptive strike to penetrate *my* defense, and hits me before I can hit her.

"I live, you die," she says, the last words I hear as I fade away. . . .

. . .

Back in Daiichi Takeda's cloud servers, well-prepared protocols are kicking in. Massive amounts of backed-up data are merged with an intricate persona simulation. Cutting-edge technology's fiery electrons firing me up like a phoenix, while my original is cut off from life. Bleeding-edge algorithms reconfiguring me as my biological body is bleeding to death.

This is the first time this is ever tried. This is proof of concept at its most extreme—if the concept is unproven, the subject dies with it. But the transition is true, and the emergent properties that somehow form my mind persist on a different substrate, exist in a new realm. My new conception is immaculate.

Shift to the fast lane
Through technology's progress
I am born again

I will return. . .

. . .

Neural networks are the backbone of our modern, cloud-based society. Neural networks running self-driving cars (minimizing traffic accidents, resolving congestion), neural networks producing the latest medicine (curing countless diseases, extending life) and neural networks controlling the just-in-time delivery drones (maximizing agricultural efficiency, feeding everyone). Without neural networks our modern society would grind to a halt, causing innumerable deaths and immeasurable suffering.

Yet, in order to perform their algorithmic magic, the neural networks must run unchecked. As they deliver their miracles, nobody knows exactly *how* they do it. The moment they are actively monitored, their true genius disappears. Like Murphy's version of the Uncertainty Principle: the more we observe how they do it, the less lateral their innovations. And the less we observe them, the more "out-of-the-box" their solutions become.

Thus, in this extremely competitive society, the competing neural networks run unmonitored. Which would be fine if the neural networks didn't have totally unexpected breakdowns. As neural networks absorb truly momentous amounts of data while performing their specific tasks—which they *will* perform, whatever unknown magic it takes—they can revert to catatonia, catalyzed by a black swan event. Black swan events that cannot be predicted by their very nature. Like the secret stealth fighters that broke down the air controller networks. Like the Manu outbreak that stymied the pharmaceutical clouds. Like the Blue Glider hype that threw off the drone delivery systems.

Hence, to prevent such catastrophic failures, the neural networks needed to be checked without being observed. Enter the Zen masters of the neural networks: human avatars like indecipherable kōans in cyberspace, invisible to the networks themselves, yet able to divine their health. Oshi no Kyo is the Zen master of the Daiichi

Takeda neural network, and as such is vital to its functioning.

> *keep the enigma*
> *don't collapse the wave or lose*
> *the panacea*

Therefore he must be protected, both in cyberspace—by impenetrable firewalls and self-learning anti-virus software—and in real life—by his Protectress, me: Chobunsai Harunobu. Based on the Onna-bugeisha of yore I am a female samurai wielding my naginata—which, nowadays, consists of much more than just the blade at its business end—protecting Oshi no Kyo from corporate ninjas, assassins, and other opportunists.

Initially, a competition was held to determine who was the best Protectress. I won, and I have been at Oshi no Kyo's side for two decades. Over time I have become more than just his Protectress. My second vocation was and is poetry, and its ineluctable power forged a mutual understanding, so that we inevitably became soulmates.

Yet, in order to ascertain that the Zen master of the Daiichi Takeda network has the best possible protection, there is a Protectress competition every year. Every year, its winner gets to challenge me in a fight to the death. In twenty years, I never lost. Until bloody Kaeyen challenged me. . .

. . .

My Oshi no Kyo does not want her, even if she truly is better than me. Let's face it, I was in my late thirties—someone stronger, faster, and better would beat me eventually. Yet we could not stop the yearly Protectress competition, as it's become a ritual too deeply ingrained in modern Japanese society. So, we made contingency plans.

Through its neural network, Oshi No Kyo had access to all Daiichi Takeda's data and projects. He surreptitiously instigated research into downloading a human mind to the cloud and now—unfortunately yet fortunately—I can say that it succeeded. I am alive again, and now protecting my beloved Kyo in cyberspace.

But it is not enough. I want to return as Kyo's real life Protectress, as well. First, I will show my nemesis's innate incompetence. Then, I will challenge her.

So now my avatar is hunting her over the Internet, haunting her gadgets, smearing her sangfroid, corrupting her computer. Softening her up, proving distraction at the moment of truth.

. . .

There is a faux attempt at Kyo's life, which almost seemed to succeed, if not for Kyo's own actions. Kaeyen was utterly ineffective during the strike, and is now facing national humiliation over it. She's on her way to defend her worthless defense before a national press event, as the new me appears in the streets to challenge her.

A shiny new robotic body, resembling me in great detail, yet leaving no doubt it's fully artificial. Details like the translucent skin of my arms and legs showing the rods, cylinders and servomotors beneath. Like the re-introduced *ohaguru* of my pitch-black, robotic teeth. Like the hate that effortlessly shines through my perfect, diamond-hardened eyes.

"*Kamaero*, Kaeyen Hiroko," I shout, loud enough for everyone to hear, wielding my ceramic black naginata, "you are unworthy of protecting our Zen master. I challenge you to a duel to the death."

In the eyes of the world, she has no choice. In the grip of centuries-old habits, she has no way out. Through traditions older than herself, before she even realizes it, she answers my challenge: "Over my dead body. Banzai!"

> *screaming in silence*
> *you will be*
> *losing more than face*

21

here comes vengeance
you will be
defiled in disgrace

The spectators retreat into the required circle with the two of us dead center. The fight begins, and oh bitch, I've forgotten how *good* she is. Any human Onna-bugeisha—hell, any human warrior, period—would be defeated by her, no doubt. With the cold eyes of hindsight I can see that my old body never could have won.

But this is a new me, risen from death like a phoenix from cyberspace, an invincible nemesis in robotic perfection. Stronger than her, faster than her, better than her. Even her best strikes, which would have pierced through the defenses of any other warrior, are anticipated and countered. She is so good—after all, this is the fight of her life—that she could've handled two or three champions simultaneously. Still, not good enough for the new me.

I give her the honor of a two-minute fight—the longest in any championship, ever—before I become the first—and hopefully last—robotic Protectress of Oshi no Kyo. In her utter despair she comes even close to actually striking me. Close, but not close enough. At the one-hundredth-and-twenty-first second I pierce her defense, dealing the deadly blow.

"I live again, you die," are the last words she hears.

About the Author

Jetse de Vries—@shineanthology—is a technical specialist for a propulsion company by day, and a science fiction reader, editor, and writer by night. He's also an avid bicyclist, total solar eclipse chaser, single malt aficionado, metalhead, and intelligent optimist. He's also appeared in *Clarkesworld Magazine*, Michael Moorcock's *New Worlds,* and *Escape Pod.*

*****~~~~~*****

Killer dApp

by Geoff Taylor

I suppose you could call it a misalignment of incentives.

This started back in the history of crypto, when everyone and their uncle was ICOing and tokenizing and retiring as a millionaire after a week. So, just last year then.

. . .

I usually parked The Car and stopped to pick up an Americano on the way to DeadEndJob every day. Aiming to get in before the 10am cutoff. I occasionally made it. The coffee would sharpen my brain a little, bring the abstract notions of programming and system interaction into a focus that was harder to achieve decaffeinated.

And She was usually there. Janeen. All flounce and colours. Just sitting in the *Bux sipping an espresso, reading a book like it was still the twentieth century.

It was weeks before I'd built up enough courage to talk to Her.

I'd put on my 'Aim To Misbehave' tee. I'd even washed it first—preparation was key, after all.

'Hi', I said.

'Hi', She said.

I left.

. . .

It took more weeks for me to actually ask Her out, but I did, eventually.

First date was at the beach. I picked Her up from Her part-time Ban-The-Whale $CHARITY gig in The Car, and we drove through the rain.

'Not great weather for a cabrio', She said as we ate our chips, watching the water run down the windscreen. A Bach fugue played on the fancy after-market stereo.

Yeah, The Car was a convertible. An old one. A boxy E30 BMW from too many years ago. Showing its age these days—new enough for three-point seat belts but built long before airbags were A Thing. Gorgeous and stylish, even if isopon was the only thing holding bits of it together. The stereo that came with it wasn't old enough for valves but that's the best that could be said for it.

'Driving with the top down makes up for it, those two days a year when it's not raining', I said.

. . .

DeadEndJob wasn't really much of a career, but the money was good. Blockchaining-up business logic processes for other blockchained-up business logic processes to consume was surprisingly lucrative, if brain-numbing. We weren't in this to move society forward, but if we could lower costs through automation, it meant fewer people on the payroll.

But now one of those fewer people was me.

Layoffs.

Asshole CEO made the trip to our office today to tell us personally. I'm not sure him Powerpointing at 700 of us counts as personal, but such is the nature of the man. Flew in on the private jet, sacked the management team effective immediately, gave notice to the remainder of us half of us were being 'let go', and got back on the private jet for home.

Killer dApp

We're used to Fortune 500 CEOs being assholes in general, but this felt like a new low.

Me and 350 of my closest cow-orkers suddenly had a lot of time on our hands.

I figured I'd do something with it. Put all this technology they spent so much money training me in to some productive purpose. Janeen and I were getting serious, and I had to do something to fill my time while She was working at the Royal-Society-For-The-Prevention-Of-Cruelty-To-Parkinson's $CHARITY.

I playlisted some Strauss and started typing.

. . .

dApps—'distributed apps'—are a decentralised way of storing and computing. . . stuff. I was never any good at explaining it, even though I could tell you the algorithms to ten decimal places. It's complicated. You'd write a bit of computer code, a 'smart contract' in the parlance, add it to the blockchain, and it would run. Somewhere. In some ways, it would run everywhere, on every node in the Ethereum global computer, but to make sure nodes were keen it was only the first node that ran it that was rewarded.

Like I said, it's complicated.

The important bits from my point of view were that it would run across jurisdictions—meaning no single government or company could shut it down—and that it could be anonymous—sort of. Anonymity in crypto was a difficult and well studied problem, but if you were careful and you took precautions, you could usually be anonymous enough.

Just as well, because my dApp was in a problematic legal grey area.

Imagine a piggy bank. Anyone could put money in the piggy bank. And that piggy bank has one person's name on it, say, Asshole CEO of DeadEndJob. If you predict the exact Date Of Death of that person, and are willing to back your DOD prediction up with a significant

27

enough stake, and you are right? Well then you get to keep all the money in the piggy bank.

Simple, right?

It sounds innocuous, but implicit in this: (1) you are able to predict the exact date of death, because you are in some way responsible for causing it, and (2) people put money into the piggy bank, because they want to make it attractive for someone to hasten the end of the target of the piggy bank.

Nasty.

Simple and nasty.

My dApp would take money from anyone, anywhere, store it securely in this global, borderless cryptosphere, associate it with whatever target person you chose (auto-creating the piggy bank, if you like), and release the funds to whoever staked the right DOD prediction.

Corrupt politician? Put a few tokens in their piggy bank. Hypocritical talking head? Add to their fund. Business leader done you wrong? Give to their piggy bank until it hurts. If their bank gets big enough, someone will be greedy enough to want the pot. Murder, decentralised. Assassination, distributed. Killing without the culpability.

There were wrinkles, of course. You couldn't just claim the DOD for someone for free, because then everyone would do that for every day, sure that sooner or later they'd be right. No, you had to put up a stake of 10% of the current piggy bank total to pick a DOD. And that could be a lot of dough. You'd only do that if you were sure. And if you were wrong, your money just went into that same piggy bank, making it more and more attractive to those in society with a flexible morality when it came to ending others' lives.

So what did I call it? I'd been mainlining Yngwie in the weeks before I met Janeen, and those playlists gradually segued me via Paganini into the more classical end of things. And so many Ethereum projects like geth and weth used an -eth suffix to show their heritage.

Welcome to dEth Liszt.

Janeen was staying over most nights by now. I didn't tell Her. She would just try and bring morality into my coding.

. . .

You needed Ether to use the Ethereum global computer, so Ether tokens were becoming more popular as an actual online cryptocurrency. Second only to Bitcoin, really. Janeen wanted to know how to set it up as a vector for People-For-The-Ethical-Treatment-Of-Cancers $CHARITY donations. I got to show off a bit, demonstrating to Her not just how to create addresses and wallets but how to do it anonymously. TMI about VPNs and RNGs until She begged for mercy. By the time we were done, Save-The-Bomb $CHARITY was already taking in funds.

Janeen asked about dEth Liszt. The Liszt had started making the real news, not just the techie stuff I read.

'It's just another dApp', I said. 'Like the ones I write, but a bit evil.'

'I thought "Don't Be Evil" was a thing for you coders', She said.

'Those days are long gone. Now it's all about disruption and market share.'

'So who uses it?'

'Anyone. Anyone anywhere. Doesn't matter if you're from a slum in Mumbai or a Valley king—your Ether is as good as the next's and carries the same weight.'

'To kill someone.'

'To increase the incentives.'

'To kill someone.'

'To incentivise someone to act. You aren't doing anything other than adding a little bit to a fund. The bigger the pot already is, the less incentive there is for you to add to it. Nobody's going to do anything if they don't have enough of an incentive, but no one person is individually giving that incentive.'

'To kill.'

'To correctly predict the date of their demise.'

'By killing them.'

'OK, yes.'

'I'm glad you're not involved.'

No sense worrying Her.

. . .

As a public contract on Ethereum's blockchain, anyone could see how much Ether was being sent to it, but the reporting I built-in also showed the names people were targeting. And there were lots of targets. Oscar winners, socmedslebs, instamarketers, CEOs, and pundits all made the Liszt, but far and away the most popular category was politicians. Nobody loves politicians, and apparently a great many people actively hate them. Hate them enough to pay money to end their lives early.

'dEthLisztCreator' was also a popular target. That was ominous. Turns out a lot of folks didn't like the idea of dEth Liszt and figured it would be good to hoist me on my own petard. The problem with an immutable program SHAd to bejeezus and merkled all the way down running on a global running outside anyone's control meant that my options for reprogramming the contracts were limited.

With so little I could do I was glad I'd taken steps to preserve my anonymity. I hoped they'd be enough— there was a lot of money at stake now. I started prepping a Bug Out Bag. Figuring out what exactly should go in a Bug Out Bag could have been a fun exercise if it wasn't for the cause.

Yeah, no sense worrying Her.

. . .

The whole Blockchain The World trend had taken off, and everyone was using Ether by now. The value of tokens mooned, and everyone holding Ether benefitted.

'Wait. Last month we got this much in Ether donations?' She said, showing me the Alzheimer's-Liberation-Front $CHARITY wallet.

'OK. . . ' I said.

'But the value of those tokens is now worth double what it was when they donated?'

'Yes. . . '

'Why?'

'Finite supply. More people want to use them, demand increases. Some people see a bandwagon and hop on.'

'But we can do so much good with this!' There was genuine glee in her voice at the thought of new AIDS-Wildlife-Fund $CHARITY projects.

'Go wild and crazy', I said.

The only folks who weren't happy were those who didn't have Ether or those poor sods with dEth Liszt bounties on their heads. Those piggy banks kept getting richer and richer.

. . .

My phone pinged me early one morning. Someone had just submitted a DOD bounty for Asshole CEO, and specified today. Interesting. I whispered to Janeen to go back to sleep as I got up.

His private jet disappeared from radar later that day, three hours after the submission was posted. Wreckage was found, the black box recovered, the investigation launched. No agency was saying anything publicly—'Wait for the results of the investigation'—but by now everyone knew about the DOD bounty. Whether it was sabotage or a bomb wasn't clear, but the intent was crystal. This was deliberate, known in advance. Premeditated.

People pointed at dEth Liszt. The dEthLisztCreator bounty increased.

The smart contract ran, the Asshole CEO bounty tokens flowed out to an anonymous Ether address.

The dEthLisztCreator piggy bank increased some more.

Seven people were on the plane when it went down. Asshole CEO might have been the target, but he took a six-person collateral package with him to the hereafter.

More money flowed in to the dEthLisztCreator death fund.

Police, crime agencies, and criminals were now all Highly Incentivised to find me.

By the end of the day my hands were shaking too much to pour me a Bush. Janeen poured it for me and watched me newsfeeding away, until She couldn't stand it any longer. She glanced at the feeds I was reading and took the tablet from my hands. We went to bed. I stared at the ceiling for a few hours.

. . .

Janeen tried making me a calming cuppa. I worried I'd hurl anything solid. She studied me over Her phone as I worked through the concoction.

Then my phone pinged another alert.

It's another DOD bounty submission. dEthLisztCreator. Today.

That was so double plus ungood there weren't words for it.

I looked outside. No activity at all. It was still too early for humans. Only a matter of time, though. Someone was apparently confident enough they knew dEthLisztCreator's identity to put up a significant bounty. I didn't know how they traced me. Didn't really matter. I'd been careful. But someone found me.

I grabbed my Bug Out Bag and Janeen, and we left ASAFP. 'Where are we going? Why? What happened?' All the questions.

'Away from here' was the best I could manage.

. . .

Janeen drove. Headed up the motorway, just keeping it under the limit as we neared a bridge. Me in the passenger seat, laptop hotspotted to the phone so I could dig deeper. I traced the DOD bounty payout address. It was the one She set up for Impoverished-Rainforests $CHARITY. Donations must have really flowed to get it to the stage where it could post a DOD bounty.

She accelerates towards the pillar, and, almost without me noticing, moves Her hand down and unclips my seatbelt.

That's where we are right now, crashing into the pillar. My head is speeding towards the windscreen and instead of my life flashing before my eyes I'm considering the misalignment of incentives that brought me here, and how committed Janeen is to Her Malaria-Without-Borders $CHARITY. They're going to get some serious Ether once She gets out of hospital. And dEth Liszt will just keep running on its own.

And I'm OK with that.

About the Author

Geoff Taylor is an old programmer based in Northern Ireland. He is currently fascinated by cryptocurrencies and really hopes no-one tries to actually implement dEth Liszt.

*****~~~~~*****

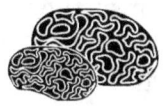

Minds Unseen

by Ellen Denton

"Good God, what happened to her face?"

The Doctor gave the head nurse, who had just come on duty and blurted out the question, an annoyed look of warning. The patient wasn't deaf and had only just been administered the pre-op sedatives. He grabbed the nurse's elbow and led her from the intensive care unit into the hallway outside.

"We won't know anything until she comes out of surgery, and hopefully, she'll have her faculties intact enough to at least write down what happened."

The nurse nodded. "Sorry I asked about it in front her; I've just never seen anything like that before."

When they walked back inside to the bed, she picked up the medical chart and scanned it for information, then looked at the patient again, who was now finally in drug-induced sleep.

"How odd is this? It says she appeared in the middle of the ocean looking just like that, wearing scuba gear, and was picked up by people on a passing motor boat who saw her surface and start floating on her back."

"It is the strangest phenomenon I've ever seen. The really interesting thing though is a verbal report the paramedics relayed to me when they handed her off in the ER. When she was found in the water, she was still wearing a full, protective scuba mask covering her entire head and face to below the chin, and it wasn't loosened or damaged in any way. Scrapings from the inside of it are down in the lab now for analysis. I'm sure the surgeons will also have pieces of things they'll be cutting off and sending to the lab as well."

"I'll bet. This is definitely one for the books."

. . .

If someone were watching a nature show about the strange and stunningly beautiful plant life at the bottom of the sea, and if that person had children, he or she would likely call them over to the TV so that they too could marvel at the educational, spectacular scenes.

Seeing these things on the National Geographic channel is one thing; seeing them growing out of a human being's face in a hospital ward is something else and is the kind of thing from which nightmares are made.

These were the private musings of one of the surgeons after he left the operating room earlier that day. He was now in the hospital cafeteria, stirring his coffee and telling a colleague about the patient.

"I'm serious. It was like something out of a creepy sci-fi movie.

"Per the reports we were given, when the boaters pulled her up out of the water, they couldn't see her face, because the front plate was completely covered inside with some slimy-looking green stuff. They thought her breathing might be hampered, so they quickly removed the head gear, and these plants that were attached to her face sprang up and outward in all directions. The vegetation had apparently been crushed down by the firm-fitting scuba mask until it was pulled off.

"So the first weird thing is, how the hell did it get inside the mask? Her rescuers were scuba divers themselves and familiar with the equipment, and said there were no broken seals or any other kind of visible damage, so nothing should have been able to get in there. The oxygen intake was also fully operational.

Secondly, where did she come from? There were no other boats visible for miles, and it was a clear, cloudless day in unruffled waters. The Coast Guard has since been contacted, and there are no reports of missing divers.

"The third oddity is that the outside of her face, underneath the plants, was *gone*. Only the meat below it was still there, with the plants attached to and growing out of that, except for one tiny, roundish hole where her mouth used to be, which is why she didn't suffocate. Every inch of her face was covered with vegetation, except for this one hole, and her airways were also completely clear with no foreign matter in them. How fricking strange is that?"

"So what kind of plant was it? What did it look like?"

"It wasn't just one plant, which might have made it more understandable—like some parasitic growth that somehow got inside her scuba gear, attached itself to her, and devoured her skin. It was more like a microcosm of underwater plant life. If someone had created a miniature version of the sea bottom and replaced her face with it, that's what it looked like. But you haven't heard the most bizarre thing of all yet. It was all surgically removed, and what was left of her head was swathed in sterile wrappings, but by the time they wheeled her back to a hospital bed, black tendrils from one of the plants had already started growing back and were poking out from under the bandages and waving around."

. . .

The medical personnel assigned to the case and two world-renowned oceanographers, along with a biologist, a microbiologist, a marine biologist, a geneticist, and an assortment of other specialists all now stood in complete silence around the bed.

The patient, who reacted to sounds in the environment, as evident by her jerks, twitches, and even violent thrashing if someone made any noise around her, had yet to respond to or show an understanding of any question put to her in any language. It was also discovered that she had only partially formed fingerprints, with several fingers not having any at all, so a check of fingerprint data bases to find an identity for her yielded no results.

She was kept under lock and key in a room set up in the hospital's research lab, in an effort to keep the people who had contact with her to a minimum. Anyone who had already seen her was made to sign non-disclosure documents. Through some miracle, the news media had not yet gotten wind of the situation.

The assembled medical and science teams were about to go into a meeting to discuss the results of the various tests and examinations done, but some recent arrivals had not yet seen the woman with their own eyes. The ones who already had just wanted to look at her again, so they gathered around the bed as well.

The vegetation had now taken over more than a quarter of her body, starting at the top of her head and moving on down her face, neck, shoulders, and the top part of her chest. On the right side of her face, a plant with translucent, silvery tentacles tipped with jeweled purple, covering that ear and traveling down her neck, waved around in the air as if moved by the currents of the sea. What looked like a black, multi-petaled rose speckled with red, tear-shaped dots covered one eye. Blue and green strands, thin as hair, undulated and flowed from where her nose and upper lip used to be, gently encircling the hole below, through which she still inhaled and exhaled. Every other inch of the top part of her was covered by plants of all sizes and shapes, some of them as common as sea grass and kelp, others never encountered before.

All of it had been surgically removed. All of it grew back, and no one knew why.

In this strangest of entities any of the team members had ever encountered, many felt the oddest, most haunting, and inexplicable thing of all was that when you placed your ear to the respiration hole in the center of what used to be her face, you could hear the sound of a distant ocean from somewhere deep inside her body, the way you can by placing your ear to the opening in a conch shell.

. . .

The team doctors and scientists had spent the last two hours sharing, coordinating, and combining their reports and information and were no closer to understanding what was happening and how it was happening. The geneticist Dr. Phil Kessinger, the de facto chairman of the group, now spoke.

"Okay, there are lots of unknowns here, so let's at least sum up what we DO now know for sure, even if we don't yet understand it.

"First, we've established, from structure and other factors, that all the vegetation is from the ocean, even the plants that have never been documented before." Kessinger glanced at the oceanographers and marine biologist, all who nodded their assent.

"Next, all attempts to remove the growth, surgically, chemically, and through the use of lasers, toxins, extreme heat, and extreme cold, have failed to produce a lasting result. The vegetation grows back, and is spreading.

39

"And last but not least, genetic tests have conclusively determined that her body is now a mixture of both human and plant DNA."

"I'd like to add something here on that." Janice Moore, the hospital's senior pathologist now spoke.

"It's as if her body has become a battle ground where a war is being waged to fight off an invading enemy.

"Antibodies, like a multi-million-strong military force, are fighting hard to ward off this invasion, but at the same time, the plants are fighting back with all *their* natural defenses to overcome this and recover or take over more territory.

"What I'm getting at here is that the plants are fighting for their survival about as hard as she is for hers. It's almost as if all these different underwater plants have colonized into a single, cooperative entity that is slowly insinuating itself into the very woof and warp of this woman's body in an effort to completely turn it into oceanic vegetation. It's not just the DNA anymore. The ultrasound done just an hour before this meeting showed actual plant substances now appearing in and around her internal organs. In fact—"

Kessinger held up his hand. "Wait. Since we've already established that these are all underwater plants, how are they even surviving at all out of the ocean?"

"That's one of the things we don't know yet. It doesn't make much sense, does it?"

Kessinger looked at his watch. "Okay, we can probably spend the whole day pondering over what we don't know or understand and get nowhere. We need more information. You all have the roster of the next set of tests to be done, with who's assigned what. Let's get those under way. To save time later, send copies of all the results to me before our next meeting, so I can correlate everything into one comprehensive report."

. . .

Before he left for the night, Kessinger stopped down in the research lab to look at the patient again. He stared unblinking at her for a long time, then lowered his ear to the respiration hole in the middle of the vegetation and closed his eyes.

The same ocean sound murmured from somewhere within her, rising, falling, almost sad, longing, and wistful in tone. He concentrated hard on it and felt like he could *almost* understand it as one would a distant voice carried on a breeze.

Based on all the information accumulated so far, he had a theory, but it seemed too fantastic to even mention to the others at this point.

On his drive home, he took a highway that ran parallel to the coastline and pulled into a turnoff to look out at the sea.

By this time, it was dark, the moon hidden behind storm clouds, and cold. The white-crested waves whipped about in a frenzy, like fangs crashing down to take a bite out of the land.

Over seventy percent of the earth is underwater. If there was ever a kingdom fit to rule, it's the sea, the last Earth frontier of great unknowns. Maybe its time has come.

His thoughts were interrupted by a chill not entirely from the piercing wind, so he climbed back into his car and continued home.

. . .

The "Patient Jane Doe" team met three days later at 4:00 a.m., on a drop-everything emergency basis; the patient had disappeared from the hospital.

When Kessinger arrived in the conference room, thick folder under his arm, he took his seat and said, "I know where she is. I was the one who took her from the lab."

Janice Moore broke the stunned silence in the room. "What are you talking about? Where is she?"

"Back in the ocean. I slipped into the lab at 2:00 this morning, when the guard went on his break, covered Jane Doe with a sheet so that she'd look like a dead body, wheeled her down to the morgue, and from there out the door to my SUV. I drove to the beach and carried her into the water, and then the current carried her back out to sea."

"Are you out of your mind?" Janice demanded. "Why in the name of God did you do that?"

Kessinger handed out stapled stacks of paper. "These are the results of the last barrage of tests done on her. For now, just read the summary on top—it explains everything."

After a few moments of silent reading, the room burst into a chorus of "Oh, come on!", "this is ridiculous," and similar statements of incredulity.

"You can read the details on your own after this meeting—the correlation of all the test results—and I assure you it will bear out what I wrote in the summary. We thought the vegetation was trying to take over a human body and turn it completely into an entity made of underwater sea life, but the complete opposite was occurring. "Jane Doe" wasn't a human fighting to not become vegetation; it was vegetation fighting to not become human."

John Harlan, the marine biologist, shook his head in disgust and disbelief, then stood up as though he were going to leave the meeting. "Are you seriously trying to tell me that you drowned that woman because you thought some form of primitive underwater intelligence somehow mobilized an assortment of "vegetables," as it were, so that they'd form a cohesive colony that would eventually, evolve into a sentient person?"

"I'm telling you yes, but that she, or it, was not drowned, is still very much alive, and that if a superior intelligence created it, not a primitive or inferior one. After all, with so much more ocean than land on this planet, do we really know even half of what may be lurking down there?"

"Is there anything in this stack of test results to support **that** little theory of yours? That it was superior?" Harlan asked.

"Not in those papers, but it's kind of obvious when you think about it," Kessinger replied. "An unknown, oceanic life form engineered the transformation of flora to human through some form of advanced hyper evolution, and further, had the intelligence and know-how to obtain a scuba suit from somewhere and get that poor plant creature, or whatever it was, into it so that it would survive underwater as a human until it got to the surface. By the time it was found there though, it had already started fighting to return to a state of vegetation.

"And one more thing, which I haven't mentioned, but which is in the report. Over a hundred more cases almost identical in behavior and test results to this one have turned up just in the last 24 hours, all in different parts of the country. Perhaps it started as an invading army of sentient sea plants made to look like people, but like the case of our "Jane Doe," and like most intelligent species, I guess once they attained conscious awareness, they just didn't want to be drafted into some war."

About the Author

Ellen Denton is a freelance writer living in the Rocky Mountains with her husband and three demonic cats who wreak havoc and hell (the cats, not the husband). Her writing has been published in over a hundred magazines and anthologies. She as well has had an exciting life working as a rodeo rider, a nuclear physicist, and an exotic dancer in the crew lounge of the starship

Enterprise. She was also the first person to scale Mount Everest to its summit. (Writer's note: The one-hundred-plus publication credits are true, but some or all of the other stuff may be fictional.)

*****~~~~~*****

Upcycling Death

by M. K. Hutchins

Death looked into the woman's shop through the street widow. Marjorie held a blue-and-white plaid men's shirt. Extra large. Her favorite size.

He leaned closer to the glass as Marjorie killed the poor thing, first taking off the sleeves with those wicked-bright scissors, snitch, snitch, snitch. She sliced what was left across the middle. From the top half, she fashioned a little square-neck bodice, turning it around so it buttoned up the back. She made a gathered skirt of the bottom remnant. With a bit more cutting and stitching, puffed sleeves finished off the dress.

Before she killed it, the shirt had been an uninspiring thing for a man to wear to an office. Now it looked like it belonged in *The Wizard of Oz*.

Death sighed. Marjorie seemed so like himself. She'd killed the shirt and made something else. Like autumn leaves becoming compost, becoming flowers. Like a tree becoming firewood becoming warmth and light. Like a human life, decomposed from all its complexity into a story for the following generations.

Nowadays, the stories were often told in statistics. Like how 99% of people with pancreatic cancer don't survive.

It didn't seem nearly as useful as the stories once told about staying away from wolves, or crumbling

45

hillsides, or keeping the firewood stocked in winter in case of a bad storm. Those stories taught you something. Made lives better, longer.

Marjorie's death wouldn't warn anyone about not catching cancer. She couldn't have done anything to avoid it.

No, the entire category of cautionary deaths—from #142 to #338—didn't suit Marjorie. He usually knew just what kind of death best fit a person, just like Marjorie instinctively knew where to cut.

The bell on the front of the shop jangled. Death jumped. Marjorie—she was staring straight at him, with those salt-and-pepper curls softly framing her face. Her smile was as warm as flannel. "You're welcome to come in and look, even if you can't buy." She stuck out a hand. "I'm Marjorie."

He wasn't invisible, but people never really noticed him unless he'd been staring at them for too long. And he tried not to stare. Death hadn't actually talked to a human since the Alamo. His throat was dry, and swallowing didn't help much.

"Umm. I'm Jim." It was the name of the last person he'd seen sent off. Eighty-one-year-old male. Alone in a retirement home. Death Type #441—A Forgotten Elder. No one would remember his story except as a number about how human social connections affected life expectancy. It seemed a wasteful way to recycle a whole life. But it was something —something the next generation could use to perhaps find happier lives for themselves.

"Well, come on in. It's cold outside," Marjorie said.

What could he do but follow? Her shop smelled like cotton and thread, with a hint of warm machine oil lingering behind it. Marjorie took her cheerful blue dress, folded it, and put it in a box.

"You're not putting the dress on display?"

"No, no. I've got plenty of stock and not enough customers. That'll be donated to kids entering the foster system. Every girl ought to have something fun to wear."

"Oh."

"I've got others like it," she said, moving toward a rack. "Gingham. Calico. Seersucker. Dresses for summer, dresses for fall. All of them with pockets—girls need a place to collect rocks and ribbons and leaves."

She didn't sound the least bit guilty about killing XL men's shirts to make dresses for little girls. "Does anyone ever get upset at you? For cutting things up?"

She laughed. "Upcycling old clothes? Not at all."

Perhaps that was the difference between them. No one wanted the old clothes anymore, so whatever she made was a gift. Dying people, though, usually wanted to stay.

Marjorie's time was almost up. He could feel it creeping up his arms, like frost hardening on a window. Two days before it burst out of his hands. He could stage her death a little sooner. Shape its meaning. Maybe a #18—Died Suddenly While Working. She could be a reminder that time was precious. Uncounted people before her, back to the dawn of humanity, had been a #18. Their collective story had inspired poets, from the writers of Ecclesiastes to Nezahualcoyotl to modern pop singers. Becoming the mead of artists was not such a bad ending.

But when Death glanced at the little gingham dress in the box, it didn't feel right. Like trying to sew on a zipper with a zig-zag stitch. Marjorie wasn't a #18. He didn't know what she ought to be.

"I. . . I have to go," he fumbled.

She sweetly waved goodbye. "Come back again soon!"

. . .

No one asked Death to *come back*. She didn't mean it. She was talking to Jim. She had no idea that after their conversations, he spent the afternoon shaping thousands of deaths.

But he had to go back, or her ending would burst out, random and haphazard like knotted-together fabric scraps. Meaningless. Marjorie wouldn't get a chance to be something *grand* after her end.

Which he could not say about the burgundy corduroy pants she'd killed. She was transforming the hideous things into a cute-as-a-button pair of overalls for some little boy. Death had sometimes managed things like that—transforming petty, cruel people into great stories with just the right timing and setting.

Marjorie was like a couture ball gown, though. However she died, he couldn't improve upon what she already was. Long before she knew about the cancer, she sewed clothes for kids who needed to be wrapped in fabric that said they were safe. That someone would take care of them.

Would Marjorie hate him, afterward? When she saw her own body, gray and limp and lifeless?

He didn't want to watch her hate him. He felt she was the one person who might understand what he did. He couldn't change the time of death more than a day or two, but he could stage deaths for a little more meaning. Just like she gave a little more meaning and use to those clothes, before they inevitably wore out.

"Hello, Jim! Good to see you back." She finished the hem, snipped the threads, and folded the overalls into the donation box.

Hello. I'm here to arrange your death. How would you like it to go? It seemed like the right, honest thing to say. But he couldn't. "When are you going to donate those?"

"Oh, I'll drop it by this afternoon."

Death #17: Dying While In an Act of Service. It was so close to #18, but to die while helping others—in this small town, there'd be a newspaper article at the least.

Given a good photographer, maybe it could go viral, and Marjorie would live on as a meme and inspire millions.

But it didn't quite seem right, either. Like making a tie out of tulle. Marjorie was quietly doing great things. She could inspire the masses, but perhaps she ought to be allowed to die quietly, too. In a way that was monumental to just a few people.

"Do you have any family?" Death asked.

"One son."

"Ah. Are you on good terms?"

"Talk to him on the phone nearly every day."

So he couldn't aim for #33—Touching Deathbed Reconciliation. But she could have a #37—Last Words with Family, where she passed on gems of wisdom to her son. Words that would resonate in his heart for the rest of his life, making him into a better man. *That* seemed like Marjorie.

"He lives close by?"

"No. He's in Korea, actually."

He could only hold off Marjorie's end for another day. There wasn't time for a #37.

She gave him a knowing kind of look. "Do you have any family?"

"Ah. . . "

"I thought as much." Her eyes were as bright as her scissors. She could see how alone he was, as easily as she saw the grain of a piece of cloth.

He shouldn't have looked through the store window long enough to get himself noticed. He shouldn't be talking with her now. He ought to leave. He hadn't caused a #35—Heart Failure Upon Realizing One Was Talking to Death—since 1256. Between her sharp eyes and how much time they'd spend together, he was lucky she hadn't already realized who he was.

"It's been a very quiet afternoon," she said. "I was thinking of closing down early. Want to get some coffee?"

"Well. Umm," he fumbled, and before he'd found the right words to turn her down, Marjorie had steered him out the front door and across the street.

. . .

Death wasn't sure if it was a date or not. Or if he even hoped it was. She'd be dead soon, and he hadn't even figured out an appropriate end for her. Marjorie was calm and easy-going, even as his hands shook on his cup.

Death #75—Public Spectacle That Brings Strangers Together. But a diner with half a dozen people in it wasn't really a spectacle. It'd probably turn out more like #85—a Very Important Conversation Starter for the mom and her young son in the corner booth eating pancakes.

That wasn't right. None of these endings was *right* for her.

On the way out, Death's suit coat cuff caught on the door and ripped.

Marjorie was on it in a moment. "Shouldn't let that stay. A stitch in time saves nine. Come along."

"I. . . I couldn't possibly trouble you."

"Of course you'll let me. And if you feel really bad about it, you can treat me to coffee next time."

Next time. It made his stomach flutter even as his ribs tightened into knots. Tomorrow—if he didn't arrange anything, she'd die tomorrow morning all her own. Randomly. Like throwing a shirt into a shredder and hoping to come out with a handbag.

Marjorie deserved better.

She pulled him back into her shop and somehow had him out of his suit jacket in an instant. She hummed as she sewed. "There. It's how it was always meant to be, now."

. . .

Death #3. Peacefully going in her sleep. Wouldn't that make a good end for Marjorie? It wasn't a splashy finish. It didn't upcycle into a memorable story. But it was the kind of thing that brought out a smidgen of gratitude. She might think, *At least it was peaceful.* Her son would certainly think it. And then he'd think of a dozen more things to be grateful for. *At least we were close. At least I don't have regrets.*

Death felt like he was cutting up a tuxedo to make a rag doll, but what better choice did he have?

He spent the night working hard on others' ends. Around 5:30 am, he headed to Marjorie's home.

But she was already gone. Awake. He couldn't grant her a #3.

. . .

Death found her at the shop. She laughed at him. "If we weren't such good friends, I'd accuse you of stalking me."

Death wiped his clammy hands on his jacket. Her mortality was a pressure, building up like creaking ice in his bones. She didn't have even ten minutes left. And there she sat, the machine ca-chunk-ca-chunking away under her practiced fingers.

"Couldn't sleep?" she asked.

"Not at all." Death never slept.

"Me neither. I felt like I just needed to get moving. Get something more done. I'm slower than I used to be." *What with the cancer*, she didn't say, but Death heard it in her voice. "Having an empty donation box always makes my fingers itchy."

She probably thought she had another week, another month—at least another day to make adorable clothes.

"Marjorie," he whispered. If he were a person, this would be a #1—Uncertainty of What Comes Next, with a lot of #2—A Bitter Parting Wishing for More Time. But what was he supposed to learn from that? He had all the time in the world. He'd still be there—he'd be the only one there—at the heat-death of the universe, when all the stars fell dark.

51

She stopped the pedal of her machine. "Sometimes, I think I can hear the clothes talking to me." She stood, leaving a half-finished romper behind. "Sometimes, I think they're scared to change. They've forgotten that once, they were cotton in the sunshine. And that one day, after they've been worn to pieces and have composted back into the ground, they'll grow into cotton in the sunshine once more."

Marjorie stepped up to him. She enfolded his hand in hers. "You've forgotten who you are. You've listened to people call you a shirt so long."

"I'm. . . I'm not a shirt."

"No. But you're not just Death, either."

He became very still. He'd spent far too much time with her—she hadn't just noticed him, she understood what he was.

At the same time, his heart fluttered. She knew what he was, and she hadn't thrown him out of the shop.

But now she was going to die. He could feel it, unstoppable, crashing down his arm like an avalanche. Her hand would go limp while he was holding it.

She smiled. "You're also Rebirth. You're Change. You're trees-becoming-tables, you're mud-into-pottery, you're compost-into-life."

She raised his hand, and pressed it against her side. Above her pancreas.

Then she squeezed. And The Cold That Stops Life rippled out of him, like thread spooled onto a bobbin. A moment later, it was spent.

Marjorie's hair drifted to the floor. But she was still standing there, smiling at him. "There. That wasn't so bad, was it?"

"I. . . I don't understand."

"You killed the cancer, my dear Jim. And from its death, I have new life."

He stared at her. He'd come to recycle her. To change her. And instead, she'd changed him—like he was any old piece of fabric on her table.

He could recall, now, a time when he thought of himself as a gardener as he broke down fallen logs to grow mushrooms and moss. As a carpenter, when he gave up dried grasses to make nests. When had he started to think of himself only as Death?

Marjorie had seen him—better than he saw himself.

She grabbed a cloche hat off her rack. "Well. It's still mighty early in the morning, Jim, my God of Changes. And I do believe you owe me some coffee."

Jim followed her out. He held her hand across the table and watched as the beans were pulverized, destroyed, and reborn as two steaming mugs of celebration.

About the Author

M. K. Hutchins' short fiction has appeared in *Strange Horizons, Podcastle, Analog*, and elsewhere.

*****~~~~~*****

Perfectly Rational Gamblers

by Henry McFarland

Signal lights warned of a possible android at blackjack table 3 seat 2. Human card counters are no big deal. Most lose a lot of money finding out it's not as easy as a book says. Some cost us a bit of money, nothing we can't handle. Android card counters with their AI can get us for a lot and fast. Those losses we can't afford.

I stood next to the flashing lights and ringing bells of a bank of slot machines—so I was close enough to see the table but not be noticed. The player in seat 2 appeared to be a middle-aged woman with red streaks in her mousy brown hair. Her green cotton dress rode up to reveal a lot of chubby white thigh. One of my undercover guys took the seat next to her. As she looked at her cards, he put a hand on her thigh.

She yelled, and he jumped out of his seat and ran from the casino. Two uniformed guards gave chase, but they knew not to catch him.

He'd had a tack in his hand. As I went over to Red Streaks, I didn't see any sign of blood from where the scratch should be on her thigh. The heavy scent of her jasmine perfume filled my nostrils. That was a nice touch, very in character.

"Ma'am, I'm Jack Davis, head of security at the Lucky Life Casino, and I want to apologize for this incident. We have that man's picture, and he'll never be allowed in here again. As an apology, I'd like to offer you a free dinner for two at our five-star restaurant, Bon Chance."

Anger didn't make her face flush or her breathing more rapid. "I don't want your damned dinner. I'm cashing out and leaving this dump." She reached for her chips. I put my hand over them.

"Silly of me, you don't eat, do you? How about some nice electricity?"

"Don't know what you're talking about." Her face looked blank. Her engineer must not have been skillful enough to give her facial expressions. The best engineers could.

"Talking about the casino rule that bans androids. Because you broke the rule, you forfeit your chips. Go tell your owner his androids can't make money here."

Sometimes the androids curse me out to make me think maybe they are human, but she just flounced out the door.

I leaned over to the dealer, a blonde with eyes a blue so pure it spoke of tinted contacts. She had to be 21 to get her job; she must have just made it. "How'd you spot the android?"

"She won a lot but didn't seem happy."

"Nice work."

"Glad to, Mr. Davis. These androids are ruining the games." Worry spread across her heart-shaped face. Androids could destroy the casino, and young people around here didn't have a lot of options when it came to jobs.

"We'll stop them." I tried hard to sound confident, because I wasn't. Thanks to the androids, the casino had lost money for two years straight. If we didn't find a solution fast, it, and my job, were gone. I had 10 years before retirement—finding a new job at my age was really tough, particularly if your old employer failed because you couldn't protect it. What could I do besides casino security? Park cars? I had a mortgage, a son who'd just started college, and a daughter who wanted to start college next year. I couldn't lose my job.

When the first androids with AI began showing up at the casino, they were easy to spot—frozen faces, no breathing. But the engineers kept improving them. Whatever we did, engineers countered. We put in jammers, so the androids couldn't get radio directions from their handlers. No radio or Wi-Fi on the casino floor. Players hated it; they had to go outside to make a call. My people hated it; we couldn't use radios and had to rely on signal lights high up on the walls. The engineers just programmed the androids to find the best games on their own.

Then we put in metal detectors. Marketing hated it. Airport-type security didn't get people in the mood to play. Players hated it, especially on crowded nights when they'd have to line up. Android engineers didn't mind. They simply used a lot of ceramics, and when they did use metal, they shielded it, so the pulses from metal detectors never reached it. Eventually we got rid of the detectors. No way we could stick tacks into every player to see if they bled. We needed a new idea, or I was gone.

Lights signaled a disturbance at poker table 1. Two uniforms held back a big beefy guy in a Hawaiian shirt who yelled at a fellow gambler, "You're a goddamn machine. You can't cheat me, robot."

A short, nondescript guy in a beige shirt stuck out his right arm and yelled back. "Feel my pulse if you don't think I'm real. Not my fault you stink at poker."

I stepped in front of Hawaiian Shirt. His breath reeked of Scotch. Alcohol is great for encouraging gambling, but it has its downside. "I'm the head of security here. You have the right to complain to a dealer or pit boss, but not to start a fight in the casino. Cash in your chips and don't come back for a month." He deflated a little, and the guards walked him over to the cashier.

Beige Shirt still held out his wrist, light blue veins showing under his pale skin. "I'm no android. Feel my pulse."

I put one hand around his wrist and quickly moved my other hand to his neck. "Tell your engineer nice try. Now get out of here, and don't try to take your chips."

A uniform escorted him out. He'd tell the engineer I'd felt his neck, and the engineer would give him a fake pulse there too, change his faceplate, and send him back. The poker tables had a lot of empty seats because players feared competing with an AI-enhanced android. We didn't get any profit from empty seats.

Next morning Chuck Simmons, my boss, called me to his office. A large man with a ruddy complexion, he glared at me with narrowed eyes that flanked a nose that was a little too flat. He'd been a professional boxer, and not a good one.

"Jack, you're supposed to be head of security, but you're letting these androids kill us." He didn't have any great ideas that I'd ever heard, but still he'd point the finger at me.

"We're doing all we can. We trained our people in how to spot them, and we catch one or two every night."

"Not good enough, you catch one, two more get through and cost us a few thousand. And they scare the players away."

"We're studying surveillance tapes of the ones we catch, trying to get better profiles to detect them. But if we find them, we have to let them walk out, and they come back with new faceplates."

"The bill to let us seize androids caught gambling is going nowhere in the legislature. Tech companies fight anything anti-android. Church ladies fight anything we're for. We can't wait for the legislature, or for you. Find a way to stop the androids and find it fast. Now get out."

My excuses hadn't convinced him. They hadn't even convinced me. Outside his office, I wiped some sweat from my forehead and wondered if things could get worse.

They could. Next morning, the central system gave me the night's report. Its flat mechanical voice made me yearn for the days of human secretaries. "Unusually heavy losses, roulette table 2."

I called up video from the camera that covered that table on one of my screens and the croupier's file on the other. The croupier looked okay: with us for years, no trouble, recent clean drug test, no financial issues.

The video showed a player putting $100 on twenty-eight. It hit, and he won $3500. He raked in all but $200, which he put on four. That hit, and he put $200 on twenty. Thirty-two, the number next to twenty, hit instead. He tried again, $200 on twenty-seven. It hit, and the pit boss went over and stood next to the croupier. The player must not have liked the extra scrutiny, because he left the table. He took $16,800 with him.

I returned the video to the point where he'd joined the game and ran it in reverse to see where he'd come from. For an hour before he'd started playing, he'd sat at the bar next to the wheel. He'd poured a few martinis down his throat, no doubt they went into a container where a person's stomach would be, and he stared at the game with more concentration than a human could muster. Over the years, people had tried to use computers to predict the behavior of roulette wheels, but smuggling a computer that could process all the necessary information into a casino had been too difficult. With AI androids, it could be done.

We'd rebalance the wheel, but that wouldn't stop the problem. We couldn't make sure every wheel was perfectly balanced all the time. The androids would keep looking for regularities and exploiting them. A roulette game where players hit three out of four times would kill a casino.

Later that day, Chuck called me to a conference room overlooking the casino floor. Below us were 150,000 square feet of games and players surrounded by colors and lights designed to make them think they were in a world of fun and excitement. How many of the players were androids who didn't care about that? Who were only looking for chances to make a big score—the poker player too drunk to play his best game, the roulette wheel too regular? That was what really made the androids different. Could we use it against them?

Chuck looked even angrier than the day before. "The damn androids are like mice—nibbling away at us until there's nothing left. If you can't get rid of the androids fast, I'm getting someone who can."

So who would that be? Better not ask. Besides I had an idea. "Yeah, like mice, and I'm going to build a mouse trap."

"If that's a joke, you're gone."

"No joke, it'll work. I'll need some help from game development though, OK?"

He snarled, "OK" and stomped back to his office.

The game development people needed some persuading, but soon the first thing a player saw when entering the Lucky Life was a bank of machines that offered a new game, WIN DOUBLE! Signs over the machines spelled out the rules in big block letters:

$10 STAKE TO START—WATCH IT GROW!

HALF THE TIME YOU WIN DOUBLE YOUR STAKE—BET $10 TO WIN $20!

Chuck and I sat in his office and watched the video feed from the camera that covered the new game. He looked at the signs, and his face turned red. "A player has as much chance of winning $20 as of losing $10. The game's set up to pay more than it takes in! What the hell is that?"

I kept my voice confident, but my lips felt dry. It was the first real test of my idea, and if it didn't work, I'd be parking cars. "Our mousetrap. Sure, the best payoff in the house, but it won't get many human gamblers. The machine is a dull gray, no flashing lights or sound effects, nothing says the game is fun. And because few people are attracted to it, there are no others around to cheer you if you win. For a human gambler, it's a bore."

As if to test my point, a guy with sparse gray hair and white shoes walked up to one machine and put in a $10 chip. The screen showed

CONGRATULATIONS YOU WON!

YOU HAVE $30 PLAY OR STOP?

He picked stop, took his $10 bet back and his $20 winnings, and shuffled off towards the card tables.

Chuck let out a great sigh of exasperation. "Great. Rather than entertain people as they lose money, we bore them as we lose money."

"That's humans. Because it's got the best odds in the casino, androids won't be able to stay away. They're perfectly rational. They only care about the money they can make, how much, how fast. You said it yourself. It's the only game set up to pay more than it takes in. Why play anything else?"

A player in a pants suit, her brown hair pulled back in a ponytail, stepped up to a machine. She had a handful of $10 chips, and she put one in. The screen told her she had $30. She tried again and got up to $90.

Chuck still didn't get it. "So we keep the androids from the other tables by making it easy to beat us here."

"No, they don't beat us. You see, because the odds always favor them, they never walk away. But every time they play, they have a 50% chance of losing. Eventually they do."

"Couldn't they just take their winnings, keep some, and start again with a smaller bet?"

"Androids won't do that because it's irrational. The game favors the player, so the more you bet the bigger your expected winnings. A human might try that, but since they have to keep the bet small, it would take a lot of time to win serious money, a lot of time playing a boring game."

Ponytail played again and lost her $90. She put in another $10 chip. Meanwhile what looked like a young guy walked up to another one of the machines. Both stayed glued to the games, obsessively playing over and over.

Chuck got up to go. "Nice work. But you know the engineers will counter."

"Sure, in a few days, they'll program the androids to identify and avoid this game. Then we'll counter—change its appearance and tweak the odds and payout. They'll probably try something else. But androids get caught in this trap because their software makes them seek the best bets. That's hard to change without making them less likely to win big in other games."

Ponytail was down to her last chip. She put it in and won, then let the winnings ride and lost. Showing no emotion, she left the game. Another monitor showed her leaving the casino. A different player took her place—probably an android.

Chuck actually smiled before he went back to his office. Sure the engineers would beat the mouse trap eventually, but by then, I'd have figured out something else. I only had to keep winning for another 10 years.

###

About the Author

Henry McFarland has published stories in the Starship Sofa podcast, *Andromeda Spaceways*, and *Every Day Fiction.*

*****~~~~~*****

The New Season

by Graham J. Darling

A sharp double toot sounded from the street outside. I rolled over and peered between the curtains: up, first, at the flagpole in my front yard, where a few tatters at the top stirred weakly in the dawn's early light; then between bushes at the rusty vehicle turning the corner and vanishing.

Then I took a minute to check over my ravaged carcass. With COVID-34, the spots were purple. They itched like blazes and left scars like bullet-holes, but at least we weren't shambling about, eating brains—that had been COVID-29.

I crawled out of bed and hand-pumped my scuba gear, then went out to get the day's food from the blue box at the curb, then flip it back over to show to whom it may concern that I was still alive. There hadn't been any recycling or garbage collection for a good ten years, but that's what backyards are for; nor was anyone still paying the farmers who came around in crop-spraying masks and biodiesel pickups, but their daily deposits of apples and beans and corn meant we in town wouldn't have to come knocking on their doors, coughing in their faces.

Then, because it was a Wednesday, I went back out and walked down the middle of the street, high-powered rifle at the ready to enforce social distancing, and maybe bag the odd three-eyed crow (their corvid COVID wasn't contagious to humans, this year, yet). From a block away, I waved at the house of my fourth wife—the one who'd lasted the longest, so far—and she blinked her shutters twice in return, and we were good for another week.

Then I came back to collect my crowbar and axe and went out to chop wood to cook breakfast. The current timber supply was starting to show its foundations, and I'd soon need to start on another. There'd be little to fear from the people inside: virus doesn't live long on corpses.

I scooped a pitcherful of water for boiling from the rain-barrel on the way back in, and that was that for my outings for the day.

After a spell of paperwork, I fired up the solar sat-phone and called my Cabinet to review the state of the nation. There hadn't been an election in years, but with every president having died in office, eventually the succession had passed to me, ex-postmaster in these parts.

"Good morning, Mister President!" shouted the Secretary of State, still somewhat deaf from COVID-24, and my own successor until I could recruit a new vice-president with their own phone, or find anyone left from Congress.

"Oh, what's the use?" mumbled the Attorney General—there hadn't been any births since COVID-31, a mumps mimic. "None of that, none of that," said the Secretary of Defense, a Churchill fan—some hope remained that very young children might yet grow up to be fertile.

The pleasantries aside, we were briefed by the Secretary of Homeland Security on what she'd gathered from her phone-in talk show. Then we thrashed out the

Middle East question for a while (whether anyone there was left), and finally moved on to the usual main course.

The Secretary of Health began there by pushing for regular check-ups (he'd been a dentist). The Secretary of the Treasury, a frustrated tax-preparer and still a bit cracked from COVID-32, repeated as usual that all carriers should be shot in the head, and the Secretary of Commerce very reasonably pointed out, once more, that this would only spray more infection into the air, and even apart from that, could only end with no one left alive.

"What I'd like to know," I said, "is what next year's version will look like. Has anyone got a clue yet about COVID-35?"

"I am COVID-35," said the Secretary of Agriculture, speaking for the first time that day.

I shut my eyes with an inward groan—insanity, again. Unless. . .

"Uh, pleased to meet you, Mister, uh, 35. So you've taken over your, uh, our colleague's brain? Any chance he'll, er, ever get it back again?"

"Avenues for collaboration may yet be found, if he lives," said COVID-35. The words were what the man we knew might've chosen, but delivered in a strange clipped monotone. "But today I must speak to you for myself."

"Go on," I said. My Cabinet all leaned forward expectantly, except for the Secretary of the Interior, who had fallen asleep—at least, I hoped it was sleep. He'd been the most spotted of any of us.

"I know my own survival depends on yours," said COVID-35. "If you go extinct, so do I."

"Then why," I said, "are you killing us off?"

"Why this is happening," he—it—said, "is because your kind has been far too healthy for far too long. Fire is a natural part of forest life, so that some trees like sequoias even need the touch of flame to open their cones and release their seeds. But if you humans start putting out every little smolder before it really gets started, then the underbrush just keeps piling up, so when the big one finally comes along and escapes control, everything gets burned to white ash: root, stem, seed and all."

I got the message, and nodded: enough with the vaccinations already—of course that's what a virus would say.

"In the normal course of things," the possessed one went on, "when faced with a new disease, those who already happen to have what it takes to survive will live to pass that on to their descendants. But the germ itself will also mutate into milder forms, that succeed through leaving their hosts alive long enough to jump to others, even protecting them by stimulating or preparing their immune systems against worse things. Thus, a guardian virus might eventually be allowed permanent residence in the human body, and even its template taken up into the human genome, much like hunters who evolve into shepherds, or bandits into an aristocracy and a State. It's that kind of co-existence we've been working towards, but you've all been just. . . so. . . easy to kill."

"I see," I said. The Secretary of the Interior had slumped right over—looked like I'd now have to find a replacement there, too. "What do you propose, then?"

"To study the precedents," said COVID-35, "by consulting our ancestors. That's why I've now summoned COVID-8341 BC from the depths of this body's chromosomes, to tell us how he and you people managed to make it through that earlier outbreak."

The Secretary of Agriculture's second head, a souvenir of COVID-27, usually didn't have much to say, but now began to sniffle and wheeze, while COVID-35 translated. "Never had this trouble in my day—you humans knew your place back then pineapple—sorry, that was an actual cough. You died when you were supposed to, so the rest of us could live and we could all just get along. Now it's all so complicated. . . The last time things got this bad. . ."

We waited with bated breath—some breaths more bated than others, if you count the Secretary of the Interior.

"I heard 35's talk of forest fires," said, arguably, the Secretary of Agriculture, COVID-35, or COVID-8341 BC. "Well, one way to stop a fire dead is to take away its fuel—to make a firebreak, by cutting out a swath downwind with axes, or burning one out with your own backfire, anything to destroy some of the forest faster than what'll destroy it all. That's what COVID-Cretaceous had to do, he told us the other day while we were all kicking back in the gene pool.

"His shtick had been to turn all the cells in a body—liver, skin, the works—into neurons. In those days, dino-brains walked the Earth. Kills 'em in the end, of course, but before they all died out, the strongest strain developed a hive mind, clairvoyance, telekinesis—it understood in time what was happening, reached out and nudged an asteroid from its orbit, and the rest is pre-history."

"My God," whispered the Secretary of Labor.

"Not really," was the reply. "But COVID-Cambrian still preaches to us on the perfect COVID of a bygone RNA World before it fell into DNA sin, and of which we are but a sorry remnant.

"But enough about us. Let's not lose track of the main issue here, or beat around the bush. Your people's population is low right now, but to break this cycle we're all caught in, it has to drop still lower, suddenly, and for years. You've got nukes: it's time to use 'em."

I did indeed have nukes: the key code I had inherited with my office, to activate and launch any part of our great nation's automated atomic arsenal, or all of it.

"What, do your dirty work for you, to ourselves? Never!" stormed the Secretary of Defense. "We shall fight you on the beaches, we shall fight you in the hills. . ." The Secretary of the Treasury was also shouting again, and the

Secretary of Education burst into tears. The ruckus was loud enough to wake the dead; abruptly the Secretary of the Interior sat up straight, blinking.

The Cabinet meeting threatened to dissolve into chaos. I put them all on hold and took a bathroom break.

When I got back from my bucket in the garage, things had already quieted down some, and I waited until I had everyone's attention again.

"While we all appreciate your coming forward," I said to our guest or guests, "and we stand ready to further consider your claims, I feel that my Administration currently lacks the mandate to carry out the action you suggest. The people ought to be consulted before we kill most of them off, perhaps in a plebiscite—"

"And cause a nationwide panic?" said the Secretary of Transportation, but we all looked at her in weary astonishment.

"—or an election."

An election! Smiles broke out and heads nodded all around. It was high time we had one, if only to remind the nation it was still a nation, with a government to look after it, and a flag and an anthem and everything. And this was an issue that was sure to capture the public interest, with more at stake than just who's left alive to rule. Namely, who'll be left alive to be *ruled*, something folks would surely take a lot more personally.

The Secretary of Agriculture immediately tendered his resignation so he'd be free to found the COVID Party and run for president and vice-president, and I was secretly relieved to see him go: we didn't want the Enemy at our inmost counsels, after all.

And after all, an election would keep it busy, keep us all busy, until COVID-36.

###

About the Author

Graham J. Darling holds a degree in molecular biology, with college credits in human physiology and population ecology, all of which play a part in this story. Publishers Weekly called "outstanding" his piece in *Sword & Mythos* (eds. Silvia Moreno-Garcia and Paula R. Stiles, Innsmouth Free Press). His other fiction has appeared in *Pulp Literature* and *No Greater Love: Martyrs of Earth and Elsewhere* (ed. Robert J. Krog, Hiraeth Books). He recently won second prize in the National Fantasy Fan Federation (N3F) Short Story Contest.

Forced Teaming

by Monica Joyce Evans

The dead are unhappy, and it's not my fault.

Three of them won't even talk to me. The fourth is Avril, and it's Avril's idea to go down to the beach. Which I guess is a good idea, because I'm not supposed to let them get bored, but I'm also not supposed to let them get excited because of bleed-through, and I can feel everybody kind of shuffling around in my Neural Lattice (trademark, copyright, proprietary blah blah, and don't say too much about it) so I probably need to go out and do something. Which isn't even my job, but somebody needed to take all their signatures in temporarily, while the expensive techs fix whatever's secretly crashing, and I was around. And nonessential.

I don't even like the beach. But Avril loves it, so we go. Least I can do, right?

I take my shoes off in the cold sand and let little waves foam over my toes. They turn blue. "It's supposed to feel refreshing," Avril says in my head.

"Wrong beach for that," I say out loud, looking out over black waves like an oil slick under a dark sky. Just a few faraway pinlights from the generators on the horizon. "I've actually never been down here."

"You've lived here how long? Four years, wow," Avril says, answering her own question. I'm mad for a second, but it's not her fault. She can't help sifting through my surface thoughts, any more than she can help spraying her own memories across my lattice: bright sand on warm beaches, incandescent leaves with the sun behind them, red and yellow flowers. "Hibiscus," Avril says.

"I know what they're called," I say, and separate as much as I can. The lattice helps, but it really wasn't built for this. Usually I store data in my head, not dead people.

Anyway, it's a waste getting mad at Avril, or any of them. It's not like they're real. The real people are gone. These are just the copies, made in the last seconds before brain death by parents and spouses who couldn't let go. At least, not in the moment, and who could blame them? Bad time to make a life choice, I think. Especially for someone else.

The waves lap in and out, oily and gross. My grandmother liked beaches too, I remember, and tamp the memory down quickly, before Avril says anything. Grandma died before uploading was a thing, and I miss her, a lot, but. . . Well, there are worse things than being dead. At least, I think so.

My bare feet are freezing, and sticky. "Look, it's not like I have work in the morning, but. . . "

Avril sighs like a little girl, and I turn to leave. "I want to see my family."

"I know," I say. "I'm sorry." There's not much else to say. I've been given strict orders not to talk to anybody. I'm also under orders to stay home, keep them happy, keep them separate, keep them calm, keep quiet, keep going to my therapist and maybe theirs as well, and it'll all get sorted out when the system's back up in a day or two. Or three.

Right.

"Can we get coffee?" Avril asks, as I head back up the seedy beach toward the little path between the reeds. "Chai latte, with ice?"

"Black," I say. "Hot. Strong as it comes." We both laugh, because of course even our coffee preferences don't match. "It's fine. I'll get both."

I barely stop in time, as he steps out in front of me.

He's big. I back up a step.

"He scared me," Avril says. Avril died in a car wreck. Her fault. No other casualties. My shoes are hanging loose in my hand. I was going to put them on when I got up to the street, had a chance to brush the dry sand from between my toes.

"I thought I heard something," he says, moving closer. "Are you okay?" He's not that big after all, just wearing a puffy coat. And a hat. And sunglasses. It's too dark to make out any details, really.

I wonder if that's by design.

"I'm fine," I say. He's still taking up the entire path. "Move over, will you?"

"No need to get defensive," he says, palms out. "I'm a good guy. Promise."

"I don't like him," Avril says. I feel the moment her car spun out of control, her adrenaline spiking, and I am terribly afraid.

"Ma'am," says another voice, one I haven't heard before. One of the other three. "Ma'am, we need to get out of here. Right now."

"Stop talking," I say to them. "Right now."

The guy bristles. I can see it in the change of his silhouette, even with the hat and glasses, but his voice stays pleasant. "I'm just making sure you're okay, that's all." He still hasn't backed up, and I can't get by him without passing too close.

"Ma'am," the new voice says again. It's smooth and cultured, and urgent. "I need you to listen to me. Do exactly as I say."

I resist the urge to touch the little mesh at the base of my neck, where the lattice hardwires in. It's just like data, I was told. Except they're conscious. I die, they die. Again, in their case. I can't imagine any of them are eager to repeat the experience.

The big guy's cocked his head, like he's looking at me differently now. Like I'm a creature under glass. Hopefully one with bright stripes that mean poison. "You're out pretty late," he says. "Meeting friends? Or just avoiding your parents?"

"He's fishing," the voice says. "Wants to know if you're alone."

"My parents are down the beach," I say, knowing I look young and letting him believe it. "All eight of 'em. I'm a blended clone."

He laughs. "You're too pretty to be a clone. I'm Jim, by the way," and he sticks out a hand. I back up a step. "Hey, now," he says. "Don't hurt my feelings."

"He's telling himself he won't harm you," the new, cultured voice says. "He'll believe it, too, right up until he does."

"What does he mean, clones aren't pretty?" Avril says at the same time. "Of course they are, if the host is pretty."

"Seriously, Avril, shut up," I say out loud. I don't have another way to talk to her, or any of them. They can feel my surface thoughts, maybe, definitely my feelings, but it's not like I can issue commands. Maybe, in this one specific instance, it helps to look like a crazy person.

Doesn't deter Jim, though. "Who are you talking to?" he asks.

"My eight parents," I say. "They're military ops. It's how they met. They're all listening in right now."

Jim raises his hands. "You got me," he says. "Guess you'll have to take me in."

76

"Go back to the beach," the cultured voice says. He has an accent, a little bit, like Scandinavian. "Don't run. There's another path up the other side."

"Bye, Jim," I say, and turn my back on him. It is really, really hard, partly because I'm getting Avril's car crash panic, and partly because of something else, like a hot blood smell, from this new person talking. Whoever he is, he knows killing.

What's that Hitchcock line? Everybody enjoys a good murder, as long as they're not the victim.

"Hey, now," Jim says behind me. "We were having a conversation." I hear his feet slap on the wet sand, catching up. I keep going, hands in my pockets. The beach is oil-slick dark, and the pinlights are very far away. This would be a stupid place to die, I think. Stupid Avril, talking me into it.

"Look at those lights," Jim says, coming up on my right side. "Pretty, right? Smart of us to come down here to see them."

If Avril says anything about the beach right now, I will kill her myself.

"He thinks he's guiding you somewhere," the cultured voice says. "Let him think it."

"I'm a geologist," Jim volunteers, as we keep walking. "Was having an argument with a friend about exactly how high the sea rise is at night, you know? Just couldn't come to terms on that one."

"He's a bad liar," my voice says. "Too many details. And he's using 'we' now, like you're a team."

"You got all quiet, didn't you?" Jim says. No way that's his name, I think. "That's not how to act towards a friend."

"In a minute, he's going to insult you. You'll want to prove him wrong, he thinks, so you'll do what he suggests. Another strategy." I clench my teeth and keep walking.

"Wow," Jim says. "You are really suspicious, aren't you. And here I thought you might be different." I can see him shrug dramatically, like I'm breaking his poor, innocent heart.

"Please," the cultured voice says. I can feel his disdain, as if he's offended my stalker is so derivative.

"What are you, a psychologist?" I ask.

"Keep walking," he says, just as Jim says, "She speaks! Hey, now, that wasn't so hard, was it?"

I can see the second path up off of the beach, better lit than the first one. Rows of apartments just past, and the street, and the lighted bus station. "Do you have anything that makes noise?" the cultured voice asks. "Anything loud?"

I shake my head. "No."

"Does anybody know you're out here?"

"No."

"No, what?" Jim asks, and laughs again. Avril's being quiet, at least. This is scaring her quiet. It feels like she's holding her breath, like the car she's driving in our mind is moving in slow motion. Bracing for the moment it hits the tree.

"Look at those lights out there," Jim says. Again with the lights. "They're never this clear. Really something to see. We should stop and take a look, you know, really take it in." The second path off the beach is in sight, and I feel like Jim's starting to walk a little faster. Like he's going to get ahead of me in a moment and block my path.

"Keep breathing," the cultured voice says. "In a moment, something's going to happen that you're not going to like."

Jim reaches out, like he's going to turn me toward the water. "See," he says. "Look at that."

"Run," the voice says.

I run.

It's not more than a hundred yards. I imagine Jim is after me, can't imagine he's not. I don't know how much of a lead I have. "Oh God oh God oh God," Avril is chanting, just like she did when she lost control of the car, and then she starts screaming, and I can feel the others now, the ones that have been quiet so far, all the fears and noises of their own deaths, a heart attack, a surgery gone wrong, the hot red knife of a violent act, and "Make noise," he says, "anything," and I start shrieking like the engines on a Mars transport, the banshee wail of a crazy person, feeling, of all things, embarrassed as I come up toward the scrubby path, pounding past the sand toward the lights of the apartment building.

I'm going to throw up.

"Don't do that," the voice says, "Find light. Find people." The bus station is empty, no surprise, but there's a row of shops across the street and one of them is a diner. Open until midnight. I scream across the street and slam into the glass door, it opens outward, and the little tinkle of the bell sounds ridiculous over my breathing.

The woman behind the counter sets the coffee pot down, very carefully. "Do you need me to call somebody?" she asks, and I shake my head no, not yet, sit in a booth and wait for coffee.

There are two cats outside, I can see, cats or raccoons, just shadows chasing, like one is the ghost of the other. I can't see anything else at all. I hunch down, making myself as small as possible, and pull the blinds.

"I'm just going to talk to myself for a bit," I say to her when she comes up with the carafe. "I'm not crazy. I promise."

She looks at me with pity and understanding. "No worries, honey," she says, and pours me a cup. She sounds like my grandmother. Grandma was a tough old lady, self-described. She would have known what to do.

I start to wonder if I should call the police.

And I start to wonder if I overreacted. If I was wrong.

"Fear," the cultured voice says, "is a gift. You're lucky to have it." My other guests are receding, somewhere back down around the edges of my lattice like they're tired, or lessened. I've never run that fast before. I didn't know I could.

"How did you know?" I say out loud.

"I have experience," he says. He sounds like a cat in cream, one of Grandma's expressions. Smug, in a way I find unsettling. He did just save my life, though. Our lives. Maybe.

Avril's not there.

"So, you're what, a therapist?" I say, hoping against hope. "Self-defense coach?"

"Darling girl," he says, and my skin crawls, just a little bit. "That's fear you're feeling now, of course. A gift, I was saying. Fear can save your life."

Avril's really gone, I realize. I can feel the other three still in there, mostly separated, and they're copies, I tell myself, just copies. Not real people at all. I've got both hands around the coffee mug, too hot, and I pull them back, rub them against each other. "What did you do to her?"

"My apologies," the cultured voice says. "I took an opportunity."

I think of Jim, reaching for me in the dark. "Nobody deserves that," I say, thinking that it's energy, it's all just energy in there, those four signatures, three now, and I was supposed to be careful with them, keep them from bleeding through, from interfering with each other, and they're not even supposed to be in my lattice anyway. "I'm just a data gofer. Nonessential." I wish I wanted chai, iced chai instead of hot black coffee, but I don't. There's nothing in me that does.

"You should call the police," the cultured voice says.

80

"For you?"

"For Jim, of course. You'll want a report." He makes a quiet, satisfied little noise. "And it will help, if he tries with someone else." He's happy, I realize, fully enjoying the situation in a way he can't usually afford, and in that moment it comes in a flood, all the things he did, all the things he wanted to do, the drive to find more sensation and do it again, carefully, carefully. Jim was an amateur. I stumble up from the booth, head to the lavatory, crumple in front of the toilet.

"How did you die?" I ask, when my stomach is empty.

"Heart attack. Congenital. I was discreet about everything else."

"Second chances are only for good people."

"Second chances are for those who can pay for them," he says. "And, of course, for those without a criminal record. We'll need to tell your employers something about Avril. A good lie. I'm very good at coming up with those."

I can feel the other two, the two that are left, cowering, staying out of the way. Three men in a boat, I think, and one of them might eat the other two.

"Don't worry," the cultured voice says. "We're all in this together."

And now I'm very careful about what I think, but a good data gofer is good at compartmentalizing. Usually, I think, not that it did poor Avril much good, but I push the guilt and grief down, and think very hard about how she wasn't really Avril. She was a new person, just a pretender. Hadn't even really lived a life at all. It's not really that big a deal that she's gone again.

There are worse things than being dead.

I fill my head with memories of my grandmother, who had a voice cadence just like the woman at the counter, who died ancient and alone, like we're supposed to, like we hope to if we're lucky, and I very carefully

81

don't think about cordoning him off, or about the sections of my lattice that aren't bearing the right kind of load, that might not survive a certain kind of jolt or disappointment or surprise. Just in case.

"Right," I say out loud. "We're all in this together." And I keep my mind closed, and wait.

Whatever happens, when it happens, it obviously won't be my fault.

About the Author

Monica Joyce Evans's short fiction has appeared in *Flash Fiction Online, Thrilling Words* magazine, and the anthology *Way of the Laser: Stories of Future Crime*.

*****~~~~~*****

The Disconnect

by Lisa Timpf

"You still playing with that thing?"

Though my partner Chloe kept her tone light, I sensed an undercurrent of disapproval.

"You're the one who *gave* it to me," I said, admiring the smartwatch clasped around my left wrist.

"Yeah. Because for the three months leading up to your birthday, that's all you talked about."

"Look, this thing's amazing—all my favorite music, my workouts, my contact lists, my emails, all in one place. What's not to like?"

"I get it." Chloe frowned. "I just worry about the lack of privacy."

Exasperated, I traded stare for stare. It was an old, old argument between us. Personally, I believed in the value of staying current. I didn't want to end up like some from my parents' generation who'd gotten so far out of touch that they seemed to resent everything about the rapidly changing culture. Besides, retiring from my job as an ergonomic engineer hadn't dulled my interest in advancements in human-machine interfaces. Chloe, on the other hand, viewed technology—no matter how cool—as a tool, no more interesting or exciting than a hammer or a screwdriver.

I studied her expression, and frowned. "There's more to it than the usual, isn't there? What's going on?"

"You remember Judy, from our ball hockey team?"

I nodded. "She worked with you at Grimmonds Manufacturing, right?"

"Yeah. Well, she works for U-Buy now. And she might be on the bubble on this round of negotiations. There's been a lot of talk about the effect of automation. The self-checkouts and now these new BrainCarts. . . "

"BrainyCarts," I said. "They're supposed to make the shopping experience more enjoyable. What's wrong with that?"

"They'll put people like Judy out of work, that's what."

"People can still choose to use a manual cart."

"The stores are pushing us toward automation, and you know it. Shaping our behaviour by cutting down the number of cashiers so people get fed up and go to the self-checkout. They'll figure out a way to do the same thing with the carts."

I scooped up the shopping list from the counter. "Speaking of stores, I said I'd get the groceries this week." As I closed the door behind me, my shoulders sagged. I'd been looking forward to putting one of those BrainyCarts through their paces, to see what the fuss was all about. But after that conversation with Chloe, it might be best if I deferred that particular experiment.

. . .

"Hello, Laura. May I help you?" I glanced around the vestibule of the U-Buy Superstore, expecting to see an employee clad in the distinctive green and gold store uniform.

The grocery cart in front of me nudged closer. "You may have heard about U-Buy's BrainyCart trial?" A melodious and distinctively female voice spoke the words. I studied the cart, which bore only a surface resemblance to the customary wire-basket-on-wheels. Built with a sturdy, metal-enclosed undercarriage, which, I realized, must contain a propulsion unit, the cart sported a handle equipped with both a scanner and a smart pad. The cargo portion of the cart had camera-eyes looking both outward and inward. The engineer in me admired the tech.

"Well? *Have* you heard about the trial?" The voice had come from the SmartPad on the nearest cart.

"Yes," I replied. I glanced around, checking to make sure no-one was watching me talk to a *cart.* "I have. But I'm quite capable of using a regular cart, thanks."

I stood on my toes and frowned. I could see the non-motorized carts, but a phalanx of the BrainyCarts formed a metal barrier between me and them. *Maybe just this once. . .*

"Fine. Let's go." Accompanied by the self-propelled cart, I wound my way through the fruit and vegetable section, selecting a bunch of bananas, a bag of avocados, a package of spinach.

"If you allow me to scan your shopping list. . ." The cart made the suggestion delicately, almost casually.

"I like to browse," I replied.

Music played softly in the background as we wandered the aisles. "That's an oldie but not-so-goldie," I grumbled. "Must have hit the peak of its popularity back in the stone age."

"Would you prefer different music? I can get your preferences from your smartwatch—"

"Really?" I asked. "Okay. Try me." Seconds later, I heard the intro for my favorite song wafting out of small speakers on the BrainyCart's handle. I grinned as we resumed our trek.

Though I'd been reluctant to use the BrainyCart, I had to admit that shopping had never been easier. Any time I had a problem finding a particular product, the cart guided me to the right location. I floated up and down the aisles, cocooned in familiar music. Even checkout went smoothly. No need to visit the cashier's station or even the self-serve unit—the cart had read the bar-codes of each product as it entered its confines. It even scanned the tags of produce items, weighed them, and calculated the cost as I loaded them into the cart.

When it came time to pay, the total amount displayed on the SmartPad seemed higher than I normally spent. Then I remembered that the BrainyCart had made several suggestions, encouraging me to buy my favorite sweet-and-salty popcorn mix as well as a few other treats. I hadn't resisted. *I'll have to be more careful next time*, I told myself.

Once I'd scanned my wrist-chip into the SmartPad, the cart led the way to the doors, rolling ahead at a brisk pace. We passed through a pair of security panels, which blinked green when they compared the SmartPad data to the radio frequency identification on the various products. Instead of going to where my vehicle was parked, the cart rolled toward the right.

"Why are we going this way?" I asked.

"You'll see."

And I did. Because as we approached the area reserved for grocery pickup, my car pulled up.

"How did you do that?"

"Push-button start, right?"

"Yes, but—"

"If you would care to unload your groceries, I have other customers to attend to."

I took the hint. Moments later, I was on my way. *What a time-saver,* I thought. *I'll have to tell Chloe.*

But my enthusiasm ebbed, replaced by a pang of guilt, when I saw the protestors gathering near the store entrance.

. . .

"Do you mind doing the shopping today? I've got a couple of things on the go." Chloe shot me a pleading look as she walked into my home office the following Wednesday.

"Sure," I said. "Not a problem." Any other time, I'd have been annoyed. After all, what's to say I didn't have stuff to do, too? Today, though, I was okay with it. We'd just had another big blow-out about the grocery store issue. I welcomed the excuse to get out of the house.

As I walked out the door and headed for the car, I mulled it over. Negotiations at the U-Buy, it appeared, weren't going all that well, and Chloe had hounded me to join the protests.

"It's not my thing," I'd said. "Walking around with signs."

"We need to mobilize people. Get them engaged. Don't you see it's a bigger issue? And these BrainyCarts are making it worse."

"I used one. Personally, I thought it was kind of fun."

"Fun?" Chloe stared at me with the same affection she showed toward the spiders that occasionally found their way into our house. That is to say, very little. I squirmed under the intensity of her gaze, compelled to explain my viewpoint.

"No bumping into other carts. Listening to my favorite music. No problem finding anything," I mumbled, realizing as I spoke how shallow I sounded.

"That's all that matters to you? Convenience?" Chloe looked away. "I'm sorry. I shouldn't have said that. It's just—I feel that we need to take a stand at some point. Against companies shoving stuff down our throats, whether we want it or not."

"It's my choice to take a cart or not."

"Is it?"

I thought about the way the BrainyCarts had blocked off entry to the cart corral where the regular carts were stored. Just the other day, I'd seen a woman head for the non-motorized carts, then settle for a BrainyCart instead when six of them surged aggressively around her.

Nonsense, I thought. *You were imagining things. You could get a regular cart if you really wanted. Anybody could.* Eager to battle back against the growing sense of doubt instilled by Chloe's words, I scowled. "Conspiracy theories. What would be in it for the stores?"

"Higher sales, because they can push certain products. Less staff, with the checkout feature."

I thought about the cost-benefit models that our company had demanded any time a department wanted to make an equipment investment and shook my head. "The carts can't be cheap. Where's the pay-back?"

"Once the stores have made the initial outlay, they'll pay for themselves, I'm sure. Reduced staff, for one thing. Quicker processing of customers. Social distancing, in case of another pandemic—you'd never even have to go near a cashier."

I pondered that notion. *Someone* would have crunched the numbers at the grocery stores, and if it didn't make dollars-and-sense, they wouldn't have done it. "Look, the cart treats me more politely than the staff do, sometimes. And you don't have to wait in line. It's really handy."

I glanced hopefully at Chloe's face. She remained unconvinced.

"The tech is pretty cool. They're self-learning, actually. What I wouldn't have given for that ability back in the day. . . "

Chloe's expression hardened. "Thing is, what exactly are they being encouraged to learn?"

This time, when I walked toward the U-Buy entrance, I had every intention of using a push cart. But a BrainyCart greeted me by name, and a friendly voice felt so comforting after the atmosphere at home that before I knew it, I'd paired up with the cart and headed toward the vegetable section.

This'll make it quicker, and I can use the time I save to polish off some of the items on my honey-do list, I rationalized. *That'll make Chloe happy. . .*

I scanned my shopping list into the SmartPad, and we made double time through the aisles. The cart even picked up some of the items for me, using its handling arm. It wasn't until I got home that I realized that the best-before dates on the yogurt containers that the cart had selected were near expiry.

I'd never have picked them with those dates. Maybe Chloe has a point.

. . .

Friday of that week, clouds loomed grey and low over the grocery store as I entered. I shivered against a cold breeze. *Better hurry. Looks like something nasty might be blowing in.* An automated cart greeted me. "I need to go to Returns," I said, brandishing a box of cereal that had, on examination when I got home, already been opened. *Another selection by the cart,* I thought, shooting it a glare as it followed me. *Well, maybe not that particular one, but still.*

As I made my way toward my destination, my pace slowed. *Wonder what's going on. There's a big line-up for something.* I craned my neck to get a look. *The returns desk.* Customers displaying varying degrees of frustration and impatience stood in line, peering ahead from time to time to try to gauge how much longer this might take. Some gave up and left. Many did not.

I sighed and settled into line, conversing with the woman ahead of me. Finally, I collected my refund on my wrist-chip, along with an apology on behalf of the store. I headed for the produce aisle.

"Grapes are on special today," the BrainyCart said.

I glanced at the display. Most of the bunches of grapes looked wilty. "I'll pass," I said.

"Oh. Well then."

We proceeded through the aisles. When we got to the yogurt cooler, the cart opened the cooler door and the handling arm was already rooting around for a container when I politely stated that I'd select my own this time. The cart's mumbled response contained an element of almost-human poutiness. I smiled in spite of myself.

"You seem a bit short today." The cart made its first conversational overture since the fruit and vegetable section.

"Preoccupied," I said. As I glanced down the dairy aisle, I noticed the unusually high number of automated carts picking orders without a human accompanying them. "There seem to be fewer people shopping today."

"I have heard some say they don't like to walk through the protestors." I'd become accustomed enough to the cart's intonations that I thought I could read a note of disapproval. "That won't be a problem, today." Now, it sounded downright smug.

"Why not?" I stopped walking.

The cart stopped too, but didn't reply.

"Why not?" I repeated.

Chloe was supposed to join the protestors today. If anything happened to her—I glanced at my smartwatch. *It's linked to Chloe's car as well as mine. I wonder. . .* I shot a suspicious look at the cart. *They're self-learning. And if they deduced that the protestors pose a threat to their success. . .*

I headed toward the exit. The cart tagged behind. "Hey! What about your groceries?"

"Put them back. Or keep them. Whatever."

Half-way to the door, I had to dodge a dishevelled attendant wearing a green and gold U-Buy shirt as she hurried past, repair kit in hand. I looked behind me. The cart, now beeping persistently, rolled a few feet forward, then an equal distance backward. "Put them back," it said, heading in my direction. "Keep them." It moved away. "Put them back. . ."

I smiled grimly and picked up the pace.

. . .

"Chloe. You're still here." I stood in the kitchen, breathing heavily after my mad dash into the house.

"Just heading out." Chloe fastened the snap on her bike helmet and started to walk toward the door.

"The sky looks nasty. Looks like a storm's blowing in."

"The car wouldn't start. And I promised I'd be at the store today, to support Judy." She set her jaw.

"About that—something strange is going on. I could give you a lift, tell you about it along the way."

Chloe hesitated. I pressed my advantage.

"Look." I swallowed, mustering the courage to say what had to be said. "I've been thinking. About this whole cart thing. And—I'm starting to think that you may be right."

A muscle jerked in Chloe's cheek. She didn't reply, but at least she didn't move away.

"I have an idea, and I think you'll like it." I said.

Chloe studied me, eyebrows lowered. "Fine." She shrugged. "Let's hear it."

. . .

As I entered the store, with Chloe just behind me, I saw a woman about my age looking longingly at the non-motorized carts. To get there, though, she'd need to run the gamut of the BrainyCarts that milled about, matching their positions to hers like blockers in a football game.

I took a step closer. The nearest cart rolled over. "Hello. Let me introduce myself. I'm—"

Noting how this time, the cart had not called me by name, I felt a tinge of hurt. When I'd taken off my smartwatch in the parking lot, I'd figured this would be the outcome. But deducing something logically and experiencing it first-hand are two different things.

91

It never really was personal attention I was getting. The carts knew my name by communicating with my smartwatch. Fine. That makes things easier.

"They're like playground bullies," I said to the woman, more emphatically, perhaps, than necessary. "Watch." I took a determined step, then another, toward the non-motorized carts. The BrainyCarts made way, moving slowly, reluctantly, but clearing a path nonetheless. Another step, another retreat. "You just need to be firm with them. They won't bump into you."

"Thank you," the woman said. She walked through the parted sea of carts.

"I get it. You're showing them that there really is a choice," Chloe said, smiling as she came to stand beside me.

"Yeah. I've noticed lots of people who didn't really seem to *want* to use the BrainyCarts, but didn't feel comfortable walking through them. This way, they'll know they have options."

"Mind if I help?"

"I'd like that."

Chloe and I spent the next three hours together, laughing and joking with the other customers as we repeated the demonstration. Some elected to use the BrainyCarts, but a surprising number preferred the not-so-smart version. By the end of the evening, we felt like we'd accomplished something. Nothing huge, but it didn't have to be. Just one small skirmish in a big battle.

Best of all, it seemed that disconnect between Chloe and I, the gap that had yawned like a chasm threatening to swallow up all the good parts of our relationship, had closed a little. Not completely. That would take time. But this, at least, was a first step.

"I'm sorry," I said as I drove home, after. "I guess I was just caught up in the whole tech-is-good thing."

"It *is* good, sometimes," Chloe agreed. "We just need to pick and choose."

"You and I, we won't always choose the same things."

"That's fine." Chloe shrugged. "What's important is that we respect each other's choices. I'll try harder to do that."

"Me too." I followed Chloe into the house, thinking about the events of the past week. We were alike in a lot of ways, different in others. Time would tell whether we'd stay together in spite of those differences, or let them pull us apart. Today, though, we'd come to agreement on one important issue. That, for now, would suffice.

###

About the Author

Lisa Timpf is a retired HR and communications professional who lives in Simcoe, Ontario. Her speculative fiction has appeared in Third Flatiron anthologies (*It's Come to Our Attention, Principia Ponderosa, Galileo's Theme Park*), as well as zines and anthologies including *New Myths, From a Cat's View, The Daily Grind, Future Days,* and *Enter the Rebirth.*

*****~~~~~*****

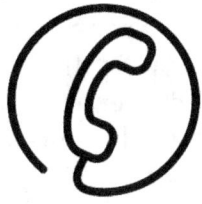

Numbers

by David Rogers

Everyone respected Miss Liza, as she was known to friends. Almost everybody was her friend. Anyone who wasn't friends with Miss Liza kept quiet about it. She had operated the telephone switchboard in the village of Red Barn Corners for forty years. So when she passed into the Great Beyond, everyone felt a loss. Reverend Wordwind spoke of how Miss Elizabeth Jane Standish represented the best of Red Barn (as ones who grew up there called it).

A few, mostly ones from Somewhere Else, said the switchboard, the whole system, in fact, should now be upgraded. Words like *fiber optics* and *digital* were briefly fashionable, especially among the young people. Soon the world's communications would be operated by machines that talked to other machines, including satellites, all by themselves. No need for humans to be involved at all. Machines that were smarter than people would operate the system. The boldest new voices said phones would someday be little things people carried around in their pockets, no wires needed, like communicators used on *Star Trek*. Few in Red Barn paid them any mind. Ones who did said, if it was good enough for Mom and Dad and

Grams and Gramps and Miss Liza, it's good enough for us. So the old system, the board with patch cords and flashing lights and party lines, stayed just as it had been for decades.

. . .

Sylvie Carter stared at the dinosaur made of plywood and fraying copper wires, the creaky-wheeled oak office chair that sat in front of it. Labels on the switchboard were faded or entirely missing, the essentials recorded for decades in the only place Miss Liza had needed them—her memory.

No matter, Sylvie thought. *I'll figure it out.*

Which she did. By the end of the second night, she was patching calls through as easily as breathing. By the end of the first week she was actually a little bored. So she brought a book, *Who Goes There*, by someone called John W. Campbell.

. . .

On the Monday of Sylvie's second week, Francie, the day operator, said, "The board's had a mind of its own, all afternoon. Probably a storm brewing west of here. Lightning plays havoc with the lines, you know."

"Mind of its own? Like how?" Sylvie asked.

"Ghost calls."

"I, um, don't know what those are."

"Oh, just static, phantom calls, like someone's trying to ring through but no one's there."

"Pranks?"

"Not from these lines. Reverend Wordwind. Judge Matthews. The police station. They don't joke around."

"So what do I do about it?"

Francie shrugged. "If it's a real call, you put it through. Otherwise. . ." Francie let her voice trail off.

"Otherwise what?" Sylvie asked, a little impatient.

Francie glanced around. They were alone. The switchboard was housed in the room off City Hall's old section, which was always deserted after five in the evening.

"Miss Liza used to tell me stories," Francie said, her tone hushed. "Sometimes after midnight, she told me, she heard voices on the lines."

"Well, yeah. It's a phone system."

"Not ordinary voices. Not normal voices." Francie was almost whispering now. "Maybe not human. At least, not *living* humans."

Sylvie must have looked alarmed. Francie laughed. "Well, it was all just stories. Like I said, probably a storm to the west. Static on the line. It's like watching clouds. You can convince yourself you see anything if you look hard enough. Or hear anything, when it's quiet, and dark, and you think you're the only one awake in the whole world. But I shouldn't be trying to frighten you, especially when you're just getting settled in."

"Oh, I'm not frightened," Sylvie said. "I don't even believe in ghosts." But her face said she did.

. . .

The call came about one, Sylvie recalled the next day, when Francie asked how her shift went.

"One in the morning," Sylvie added, vague indignation in her voice. By then she had started to feel, not like the only one awake, but as if she were the last living person in the world. So at first she felt glad to talk to anyone. In Red Barn, decent folk were asleep by ten. Calls later than that were rare, mostly coming from the west coast, where they didn't know how to keep good time. Or the rare emergency. It had been suggested that a night operator was not needed at all, but of course people quickly pointed out that *something* might happen, without mentioning fires and heart attacks. No point borrowing trouble, but better safe than sorry. Everyone knew it was so. If a cliché was true, nobody questioned it but fools and children.

"So I said, we have no such number," Sylvie said. "And I disconnected."

"What did the caller sound like—man or woman? Young or old?" Francie wanted to know.

"Man. Not a kid. Not old, but older, I'd say. Older than me, I mean."

"Where was he calling from? Was there another operator on the line?"

"No, just that voice. And it sounded. . . far off. I asked him where he was calling from, but he wouldn't say. Just repeated the number. That was when I disconnected. I mean, the lines have to be kept open in case there's an emergency, right? After that, it was all quiet. Very quiet."

Sylvie thought of the phrase *pregnant silence*, which a certain kind of writer liked to use to build suspense. It turned up often in old-fashioned romance novels. She'd always thought that language was a way to cheat, but now she found it described very well the spaces between the hum that faded in and out and the occasional crackle of faint static. And still the voice did not tell her where it was calling from. She didn't say all that to Francie, though.

"Of course. You did the right thing," Francie said. "There's always a joker or insomniac somewhere who wants to call the operator and talk about nothing."

"Well, he called again. And he asked to speak to Miss Liza. I told him that wasn't very funny, not with the grass not even grown over her spot in the cemetery yet."

"Maybe he didn't know she had passed on," Francie said.

"Oh, he knew," Sylvie said. She could not have explained how she knew that he knew. But she did. "So then he asked to be connected to another number, an exchange nobody around here ever asks for. I couldn't even find it in the books."

"What was the number?"

"314 159 2653," Sylvie said promptly. For some reason, she couldn't forget it.

"Hmm, that sounds familiar. Not sure why," Francie said. "But it's not for anywhere near here."

"That's what I told him. He kept insisting, almost rude. So I asked if he was trying to make an international call. He just laughed and hung up."

. . .

The next night, the Voice from Nowhere, as Sylvie came to think of it, called back. "Do you know what happens when someone dials a phone?" the Voice asked, without preamble.

"Who is this?" Sylvie demanded. No answer.

"Listen, Mister," she said, "it's illegal to make prank calls to the operator. Are you trying to reach a number?" Sylvie was not sure about the legal point, but she had a vague notion she was right.

Undeterred, the Voice went on. "Each time you pull your finger around, you harness a little current of electricity. You generate a tiny bolt of lightning. And you unleash it. That lightning is sent out on the lines. Where does it go?" The Voice paused, as if waiting for an answer. Sylvie started to respond. Maybe if she kept him talking, he'd let something slip. Maybe she could find out who he was, where the calls were coming from. But before she could decide what to say, the Voice went on.

"Electricity has to go somewhere. It cannot just disappear. That's a scientific fact. A matter of physics. Energy never vanishes. It's still out there, somewhere, forever. Every call ever made. Every number ever dialed. They never die. So where do they go? They cannot simply cease to exist. The laws of physics forbid that. Energy and matter can be transformed, but never destroyed."

"Right." *So what do you want me to do about it?* she almost asked, but instead said, "Give me your name, please."

"Someone here wants to talk to you. She will call tomorrow night."

Silence ensued, the deep silence of the void. Shortly the ordinary hum of the line returned.

The next day, Sylvie told no one, not even Francie, about this call.

. . .

By the end of her second week, Sylvie was beginning to adjust pretty well to long nights and sleeping in the daytime, but she found coffee and spine-tingling stories could do only so much to keep drowsiness at bay. So she brought her little transistor radio along. Stations faded in and out, but at least fiddling with the tuner kept her hands busy and her eyes open.

Sylvie tried to decide what she felt as the Sun went down and the room darkened. She got up to turn on lights and close the blinds. The little parking lot behind City Hall was empty, and again she had the feeling of being the last person in the world.

Time passed. Sophie read Edgar Allan Poe's "MS. Found in a Bottle" and listened to a radio station that played old jazz records.

. . .

The Voice called again, of course, this time at four past midnight.

"Operator," Sylvie said.

"Long distance from—" the Voice said, a blast of static blotting out the origin of the call. "Please hold while I connect you."

That's supposed to be my line, Sophie thought, but the rattle and click in the headset grew so loud, she pulled the speaker away from her ear till it quieted. "I finally got through to the number you did not connect me with," the Voice said.

"What number?" Sophie asked, as if she'd forgotten. "What operator connected you?"

100

"There are other operators than you," the Voice said.

"What operator?"

But the Voice only repeated, "Hold while I connect you."

"Hello, Dear," a woman's voice said. "Are you treating my board kindly? And with respect?"

"Who is this?" Sylvie asked.

"Oh, you know who I am, Sylvia Thomas. How many of your calls with that Franklin girl, when you were fifteen, did I to pretend not to notice?"

"Who was the man who just called?"

"Oh, he's nobody," the woman's voice said. "Well, everybody's somebody. He helps out with newcomers. Tries to help people adjust. Not exactly nobody, and really very kind. Thinks he's in charge, though nobody elected him. I used to talk to him now and then, when I ran the board. Has he been bothering you?"

"I don't know—"

"Anyway, don't let him distract you. A lot of people depend on you, you know."

"Who is this?" Sylvie demanded.

"You know very well who I am."

"You *sound* like Miss Liza. Which is not funny at all. Mary McCarthy, if this is your idea of a joke, I'm going to report you."

"You have done your due diligence, Dear," the woman's voice said. "A good operator puts up with no nonsense. I remember the first call I got from Beyond. Like it was yesterday. I did not believe it, either. Not at first. But you are part of a web, now, a net, a system so big, so far-reaching, you cannot imagine. You have to respect the system, and demand others respect it too. But I called to tell you something, and you must listen. It's important."

"I'm going to disconnect you now, Mary."

"All right, I'll prove I'm Miss Liza. Pull out the middle left drawer of the desk. Look in the very back."

Sylvie would later think back to that moment as the turning point. If she had hung up instead of opening the drawer, what difference might it have made? But her right hand paused, halfway to disconnecting, and her left reached for the drawer.

"Pull it almost all the way out, till it's about to fall. Look behind the back panel. There's a little secret space there, with half a pint of very good gin. It's yours, now. I know how long and lonely some of those nights at the board can be."

Sylvie looked at the back of the drawer, now canting dangerously downward. Sure enough, a small bottle of Bombay Sapphire was tucked away in the corner.

"That proves nothing. Anybody could have put that there."

"Anybody didn't, though. I did. But enough of that. I really need to tell you something." Miss Liza's voice—if it was Miss Liza, and Sophie was certainly not convinced—dropped to a whisper. "There will be a tornado. It will hit Red Barn."

"When? Where?" Sylvie asked, in spite of herself. *Summers*, she thought, *there are always tornadoes somewhere. And earthquakes, and fires. . . .*

"I'm not sure when. Not yet. In fact, I'm not even supposed to know. They don't share sensitive information right away with newcomers. The temptation to interfere is too great, they say. We're supposed to concentrate on letting go. Let the living deal with things on their own. But I've made some friends who know things. I was always good at making friends, just like you."

"What will the tornado hit?" Sylvie asked. *I'm daring you to prove this is not a very bad joke.*

"That's just it, Dear." The voice of Miss Liza dropped lower still. "The school. I know it will hit the school. That's why I had to tell you. What if the children are all there?"

"There's nothing I can do—"

"I know. You have to know when. I'll call you when I find out. They may punish me for telling, but—"

Another sudden blast of static, followed by a sound of scuffling.

Then silence.

"Who are *they*?" Sylvie asked the silence, and got no answer.

Sylvie poured a capful of the gin in her coffee and pondered. How could you punish a ghost who told secrets to the living? And why?

She finished her coffee, poured a refill, added another capful of gin, and continued wondering. By dawn, she still had no answers, except to tell herself it was all a bad joke, which she found increasingly hard to believe.

Otherwise, it was a quiet night.

. . .

Sylvie told no one about the call. No point in being labeled a lunatic. *What would I say? "There will be a tornado. A ghost told me. At least, I think she was a ghost. No, she didn't say when."*

The twister came the very next afternoon. The biggest anyone in Red Barn had ever seen. Everyone said so. The school would have to be rebuilt entirely, but no one died. Just good luck—or the hand of Providence, Reverend Wordwind insisted—that it came at 4:30 in the afternoon, when even the janitor had gone for the day. *Providence,* the Reverend repeated whenever the subject came up. Sylvie figured she was not alone in wondering what Providence had against schools, even empty ones, but she was too polite to ask. Those kinds of questions were frowned on in Red Barn Corners.

The switchboard was busy that evening, relatives from all over the country calling to check the safety of family and friends, get news, and gossip. By one in the morning, things slowed. Sylvie ate her midnight snack—still refusing to call it lunch—and waited for a call from a ghost.

It never came. When dawn started to lighten the sky, Sylvie poured a cup and a cap, as she started to think of gin and coffee, stored the still nearly full bottle in its spot in the back of the drawer, and said, aloud, "Here's to you, Miss Liza. Wherever you are. Hope you didn't get in too much trouble."

About the Author

David Rogers's poems, stories, and articles have appeared in various print and electronic publications, including *Star*Line, The Comstock Review, Atlanta Review, Sky and Telescope,* and *Astronomy* magazine. His latest work is *Roots of the Dark Tower: The Long Quest and Many Lives of Roland,* available from Amazon. More about David and his work can be found at Davidrogersbooks.wordpress.com

*****~~~~~*****

Bad Connection

by M. Richard Eley

Jester_333 dropped an "Is your meeting boring?" meme into the encrypted chat box and hit send. The other hacker replied with a laughing Buddha GIF.

"Check u 2morrow," Jester typed. "Got 2 go."

"Where 4 2?"

"Hack couple feeds, Zoombomb sum losers."

"Noice. L8r."

Jester ended the chat and initiated a network scan for teleconference data streams. Nowadays, all were encrypted, but the algorithms he wrote for his mesh network of PCs could crack any password under twelve characters.

In eighteen seconds, the first decryption factored out.

Legion. Such a stupid password. He shook his head in disgust. Serves them right to get bombed. Jester looked through his list of file folders, deciding which porn collection would be the most fun to flood the group with. He opened his favorite batch of photos, always good for ultra-shock: *Bestiality & Grandmas.*

He pulled on an L.A. Rams ballcap and tugged it low to shade his face. After numerous hacks, he had found it best to join a conference with his camera on, act like he happened to be late to the meeting, in case they had a suspicious moderator. If he laid low for a few minutes, he could bomb the feed with porn and watch the reactions. Playing his part, of course. "What the hell is that?" he'd exclaim with false outrage. "Somebody's hacked the meeting!"

Nobody ever caught on. By the time the host ended the conference, Jester would've flashed dozens of seriously twisted photos on everyone's screens.

He punched in the meeting's ID and password and waited to join. The app window flashed "Connecting." He chuckled.

The conference started with only one image onscreen. Not unusual, lots of meetings did that. Always some blowhard boss wanting to be in the spotlight.

Jester had to acknowledge, though, that the background of flames and smoke was cool. He'd search for the clip later, use it himself sometime.

He clicked the grid-view button, and the screen changed into an array of postage-stamp-sized images. He was the only one not wearing a costume. In a sea of demonic masks, his face stuck out like a fur coat at a PETA meeting.

Just his luck to stumble into some stupid cosplay convention.

The audio changed from an indecipherable babble of gibberish to dead silence. After a second, the conversation restarted. This time he understood the voices.

"Is that a man?"
"Human?"
"How dare a mortal disturb us."
"Wait till HE finds out."
"Forsooth!"

Jester shook his head. He had nothing against cosplay, he grokked it. But Christ. . . these bozos were way too much. He decided not to bomb them, but before disconnecting, he needed a little fun. He leaned toward the mic and spoke in a deep voice.

"I am the great and powerful Oz, and I hereby grant all of you the gift of life. So, go get one. Sheesh."

As he moused over to the "leave meeting" button, his display returned to the full-screen flames image. A metallic face now filled it. In full demon makeup, yet. As good as any big-budget movie effects. He had to admit, it looked super cool. The mask had cracks all over it, and through each gap shone a dull red glow. Probably from a video filter app, he didn't see it being a practical effect. And the wisps of smoke from the nostrils, little curls crawling up. . . way too cool.

He let go of the mouse and sat back. Got to give cred where rightfully due. "Yo, dude. That's a wicked awesome outfit."

The golden face tilted to one side and stared back. The sensation of being deeply and thoroughly inspected permeated the feed, piercing right through Jester.

"Just thought I'd say, I mean. . . ah, nice work."

Jester winced as a deep and guttural voice boomed from the speakers. "Why have you intruded into our convocation, human?"

Man. And people say hackers are nerds. These freaks don't just take the cake, they bring the bakery along with it. Jester moved his cursor back to the "leave meeting" button.

The onscreen character raised a four-taloned claw and squeezed it into a fist.

All feeling drained from Jester's body. He willed himself to click the button or slide the mouse sideways an inch. None of his muscles even twitched.

"What the hell?" His voice worked okay. He swiveled his head a few inches left and right, moved his eyes around. Nothing else functioned.

"You haven't answered my question, human." The claw lowered. "Why did you interrupt our business meeting?"

Jester had no other option than to reply. "I was just having some fun. Sorry. Could you do me a favor and call 911? I can't move."

The masked face laughed with a sound like a thousand screams of terror. It sent cold chills up the back of Jester's neck.

"You interrupted our business for. . . your amusement?" The golden head gave a slow, side-to-side shake. "What hubris."

"I'm having some medical problems. Could you—"

The face of a blue-skinned woman with pointed ears leaned into the view. In a husky voice she said, "I do not believe the mortal fully understands his error, my lord."

"Ah." The demon face gave a slight sideways nod. "Always the observant one, Lempo."

The blue creature withdrew.

"This is just a simple mistake," Jester said. "I'd have already exited, but a stroke or something paralyzed my arms, and I can't—"

"It is no stroke, Jeremy Govin. I am merely holding you until I decide how best to proceed."

"What? How did. . . look, you need to call—"

The claw came back into view and did a fast, back-and-forth wave.

Jeremy slapped himself in the face, hard. Then again. Metallic saltiness filled his mouth. He blinked away the tears.

"Do not presume to command me, human." The demon face studied him for a second. "If you do not recognize me, the fault may be mine. My old visage became tiresome, so I adopted this newer one. I discovered it in an Austin costume shop. Perhaps one of my old forms?"

Golden skin lost its luster and changed to bright red. Six-inch horns sprouted from a smooth, hairless scalp. A perfect nose flattened into two ugly slits. Bright-green eyes faded to gloss black.

Jeremy yelled, "Jesus Christ!"

The creature threw back its head and hooted, its mouth full of jagged fangs. "Oh, my. I haven't laughed that hard in millennia." It wiped black tears from its cheeks. "No, I'm not Yehoshua. I know him, though. Likes to play Scrabble."

"You're the. . . *devil*?"

"No one here actually calls me that. I prefer Lucifer, has a more poetic ring to it." He leaned toward the camera a bit. "You know how that whole devil thing started?"

Jeremy shook his head.

"Long ago, Beelzebub and I were having a bit of sport, throwing souls across the river into Hell. A Greek woman had just arrived, and she stood nearby, observing us. The Greek for 'throw across' is *diaballein*, in Latin, *diabolos*. Her idle gossip spread the word. Centuries later diabolos became devil in old English. Irritating."

"Yeah, bad nicknames suck." Jeremy tried a sympathy play. "In school, one kid used to call me Germy Jeremy all the time."

"Ah, yes. Herbert Bland." Lucifer nodded. "I expect he will end up here, if that is any consolation. My particular Greek has had four-thousand years to consider her error." Lucifer grinned, clicking his sharp teeth together. "Time to time, I like to remind her of her mistake."

"Please let me go. I promise I won't bother you again. I'll never even say 'devil' again. Okay?"

"No, I think not. Although I appreciate your penchant for sowing chaos, you have managed to infiltrate our most sacrosanct of gatherings. If I were to release you, you might share your methods with others. Just imagine the inconvenience."

"It's not my fault!" Jeremy wanted to pound the desk, but only managed to raise his voice. "You guys used a weak password. Anybody could hack such a stupid. . . uh, I mean, come on. *Legion* for a password? Really? It didn't even include a number."

Lucifer's hairless brow raised. He glanced to one side. "Did Allison schedule this meeting? Get her on. *Right now.*"

The screen split into two images. A wiry-haired woman in thick glasses and a bulky sweater said, "Yes? What is it now?"

"I am told by my good friend Jeremy here—" Lucifer gestured at his camera. "That our meeting password is weak and easily. . . what was the word you used?"

Jeremy said, "Hacked?"

"Yes, that's it. Our password is easily hacked."

Allison's eyes shifted back and forth faster than Jeremy believed possible. Her jaw twitched as she spoke. "It's your dumbass minions that keep forgetting the complicated passwords. I had to keep things simple or—"

"Thrice you have disappointed me, Allison." One of Lucifer's claws raised and pointed. "You are dismissed from your position."

"You can't be—" Her sentence morphed into a painful wail as the top of her head frosted over in white. The ice line crept down. When it reached her neck, her screams choked off.

After a few seconds, Lucifer flicked his talons, as if flinging away water droplets. Allison's body exploded in a cloud of red snowflakes. The dual image reverted to a single view of Lucifer.

Jeremy swallowed hard, trying to find a drop of moisture in his now desert-dry throat. "Hey, look, how could I know you teleconference? Aren't you guys supposed to use spells, or pentagrams? Stuff like that?"

"Until recently, we did. Back when we had a few hundred million souls here, everything was easy. Nevertheless, one must change with the times. We service billions now. And as I'm sure you're aware, documents can't be transferred through pentagrams. Couriers must carry them. Takes resources, you see."

"Right, so, I don't want to hold you up. If I—"

"You know how much space it takes to store all that parchment? Hmmm?"

"I. . . no, not really."

"Why, it's the size of—" Lucifer spread his claws apart, then lowered them. "Where do you hail from, Jeremy?" Lucifer glanced up for a moment. "Ah, yes, Bangor. Well, picture a warehouse the size of Maine. And that's just the section for politicians!"

"Wow, that's pretty big. Hey, if you don't mind—"

"Imagine my delight when we learned that a photo of a blood covenant was just as binding as original parchment. So much easier to store JPEGs, you'll agree."

"Sure." He tried to offer a sincere smile. "Well, I'll let you get back to your work now."

"Funny you mention that. It appears we've recently had an opening in our I.T. department. So, on behalf of all of us here—" He lifted a claw, one talon extended vertically. "—and we are legion—" He grinned. "Welcome to the team."

"What?" The implication sank like a dagger into Jeremy's chest. "No, no, I can't, I mean. . . "

Lucifer crooked his talon, beckoning. "Come, Jeremy. Join us. Pick up that black marker on your desk."

A strange sensation crawled into Jeremy's arm. He watched, unable to stop, as he picked up the felt-tip pen. With his thumb, he popped off the cap.

"Well done! Now, you must draw something for me. Like this..." The talon went up, down, up, down, then around.

Jeremy's hand moved to the monitor. He traced out a pentagram on the screen, then drew a circle around the symbol. Inside the shape, the image shifted into rolling sheets of red-hot lava.

"I'm not signing any covenant thing." He shook his head no. "So, you can just piss off."

"No need to sign anything, Jeremy, you're already prequalified. Now, be quiet."

At the command, Jeremy fell silent.

A scaly, four-taloned claw emerged from the monitor-pentagram and reached across the desk.

Jeremy screamed in wide-eyed horror, but all that came out was a strangled croak.

The claw grew larger and larger. It enveloped Jeremy and the chair, fully engulfing both in smoking, red flesh. Then it shrank, compressing to its original size as it withdrew. The pentagram faded, leaving only a blinking dialog box on the screen:

> **Thank you for making**
> **Legion Communications, LLC**
> **your teleconference choice.**
> **Were you satisfied with your call?**
> **If not, please contact our**
> **I. T. department for assistance.**

###

About the Author

M. Richard Eley writes sci-fi, horror, fantasy, creative, and instructional non-fiction. His work appears in the Virginian-Pilot newspaper, *Issues in Science and Technology* magazine, an Owl Creek Press SF/F anthology, and a forthcoming Fahrenheit Books sci-fi anthology. Three of his short stories have won multiple prizes in writing contests. His current projects are a book on the craft of modern writing, a short story collection, and one or two sci-fi novels.

*****~~~~~*****

A Sweet Smell of Sheep

by Maureen Bowden

My name is Oenone. I'm a nymph. My late ex-husband, Paris, son of King Priam, of Troy, was a good-looking boy but a bit of a cod piece. Pardon my language. When he was born, his mother, Queen Hecuba, had a premonition that he was trouble. She summoned Agelaus, the local hit-man. Shepherding was his day job, but it doesn't pay well. She handed over the baby. "Get rid of him, or we're all doomed."

Hit-man or not, Agelaus had no enthusiasm for infanticide, so he took the baby home to Mount Ida, raised him and schooled him in the art of shepherding. History blames Paris for the Trojan War, but it was me that was trouble, not him. This is what really happened.

When I met him he smelled of sheep, but I didn't care. We fell in love and were married. He wrote me poems. "Oenone, oh Oenone, sweet as a peony."

I soon grew tired of him. Paris, oh Paris. You did me embarrass.

I hate to see a man cry, but how to get rid of him without hurting his feelings? I appealed to Rhea, the goddess I serve. Well, not exactly serve. I don't do anything for her, but I occasionally ask a favour of her, and she usually obliges. I told her the problem.

"Tricky one," she said. "Leave it with me. I'll consult Eris, goddess of Discord. She's good at this sort of thing."

The story's well documented. Eris chucked a golden apple inscribed 'For the Fairest', onto the buffet table during an Olympian ambrosia and nectar soiree. A catfight ensued between Hera, Athena, and Aphrodite, resulting in scratched faces, broken nails, and dishevelled tresses resembling an explosion in a cushion shop.

Zeus bundled them off to Mount Ida and placed the apple in Paris's sticky palm. The bribery and corruption began. He was impervious to Hera and Athena's respective offers of power and wisdom, but when Aphrodite mentioned the most beautiful woman in the world his lustful little eyes lit up. She got the apple. It was bye-bye Oenone, and off he trotted.

Rhea turned up a month later. "Happy now, Oenone?"

"Delirious. Thanks. What's new with Paris?"

"All's going to plan. Crack open a bottle of your home brew, and I'll spill."

I filled our goblets with my speciality nettle wine, much prized at Dionysian razzles, and listened. "King Menelaus of Sparta and his brother King Agamemnon of Mycenae had been itching for years for an excuse to plunder Troy. Rich pickings there. Eris nudged them into hatching a plot. Menelaus invited King Priam to send Paris to Sparta for diplomatic talks, whatever the Hades that means." She sipped her wine and nodded her approval. "Where was I? Oh yes, Menelaus. He pimped out his wife, Helen, the most beautiful woman in the world, allegedly. She and Paris eloped, and a thousand ships were launched to bring her back, after the Greeks had plundered to their heart's content. Mission accomplished." She emptied her goblet in one gulp. "Fill her up, girl. I've got a thirst on."

I replenished her tipple. "What's Helen like?" I asked.

"Bottle blonde, plunging neckline and split in her robe converging in the vicinity of her navel. She's a fun-loving floozy, happy to go with the flow, and while she was strutting her stuff Menelaus was packing her bags."

"Happy families," I said.

"Yep. Meanwhile, in Mycenae, Clytemnestra, Agamemnon's wife, was packing his. The sooner he was off to Troy the better. Her fancy man was chaffing at the proverbial bit."

The war dragged on for years, of course, and ended with a bloodbath. The last time I saw Paris he came crawling to me, bleeding all over my boudoir. "Help me, Oenone," he whimpered. "The arrows were poisoned."

"Sorry," I said. "I'm all out of antidote. Crawl back to Helen and rip off her scanty robe to bandage your wounds. It's all it's fit for anyway." Harsh, I know, but I had to appear the wronged wife so I wouldn't hurt his pride. I doubt if he made it back to Helen.

So, where did the wooden horse come into this? No idea. Even the Trojans couldn't be that stupid. Maybe Homer made it up. Poetic licence or some-such.

As for me, I fell in love with another shepherd boy. Golden curls and the face of a god. He smelled of sheep, but I didn't care.

About the Author

Maureen Bowden is a Liverpudlian living with her musician husband in North Wales. She has had 130 stories and poems published, and was nominated for the 2015

Pushcart Prize. In 2019 Alban Lake published an anthology of her stories, "Whispers of Magic."

*****~~~~*****

The Incredible Machine

by Dennis Conrad

Mutterings about the Incredible Machine had been spreading for months, years even. Yes, there were many machines in this city; smoky things, pump-fueled, loud, clanking and screaming. You could barely walk without running into some sort of shuddering, steam-driven thing. There were the black-sided locomotives, grand steam-wheeling ships, sputtering automobiles blowing great clouds of smoke with every movement. But the Incredible Machine was something else entirely. The sort of mechanical miracle that few believed in or trusted anymore. It would cross vast distances in the blink of an eye. A grander thing, even, than a flying-machine; for wonderful as a flight would be, it still requires time, still exposes the traveler to the whims of the worldly elements. And of course, how many ships do you know of that vanished into those harsh mists between the continents, swallowed up by whatever ocean's fit happened to cross its path? But the Incredible Machine—it was different. It would cross vast oceans in the briefest span, with the occupants feeling only the lightest tousle. No more laborious ocean-crossing journeys; if the Incredible Machine functioned, it would usher in a new world, an endlessly linked extension of this industrial age.

So, when that bright day dawned, when the Incredible Machine was announced as ready to be unveiled at the week's conclusion, the atmosphere was mixed. The people of the Gilded District rejoiced; those of the Historical District carried themselves with a guarded anticipation; and the Factory District was torn between those who felt joy in scientific progress and those who raged against the waste thrown into such projects rather than the people's welfare.

The Laboratory which the crowd gathered outside of looked like a factory itself, a great concrete slab with a towering black gate. Not all of the smoke that issued forth from the stacks was just soot-darkened, but glowed in strange greens and dark, stormy purples, as if with an otherworldly heat. The people were held back by a great cordon of police, who stood before the assembled crowd with clubs at the ready, keeping them away from the vast, empty dais which the Machine would soon sit upon. Many looked strangely upon the huge rail, made to accommodate an engine far larger than any seen prior, leading out from the huge gateway.

Some cheered as the much smaller side doors came open; others jeered. The first to exit the building was the doorframe-darkening figure of Winston Roberts, the crown jewel of the Gilded District. An entrepreneur who'd bankrolled the vast recent advancements in steam power and alchemical research, it had been his bottomless vaults which had financed the production of the Machine. He towered like a vertically stretched-out walrus, great bushy moustaches curling round the cigar which was seemingly never absent from their place between his gravestone teeth. His eyes were shadowed by the brim of a long-stemmed top hat, a comical exaggeration of his imposing frame.

The Incredible Machine

The next to come forth was more akin to a praying mantis, stick-limbs snapping as he scuttled his way through the door. This was the main mind behind the Machine's invention, the great Walter Githens, an eccentric celebrity scientist known for his wild ideas which were just as often successful as unsuccessful. Indeed, in the crowd, there were more than a few old spurned students and jealous rivals amongst the jeerers, hoping to watch a spectacular failure in the public eye. Doctor Githens blinked great bug-eyes that seemed to leave the boundaries of his head behind his thick, reflective spectacles, puffing on a long-stemmed pipe as he joined the massive Mister Roberts at the podium.

The last form to come forth got the least vitriol of all, though still an odd cry of "class traitor" could be heard. Joe Peterson, the representative of the worker's union which had been hired to build the thing, gave a curt nod to his assembled men gathered at the back of the crowd. A taciturn, strong-limbed man, with an unashamedly five-o'-clock-shadowed jaw and glittering, piercing eyes, he chewed tobacco, and idly spit a gob into a hastily-proffered pan courtesy of one of those unnamed unseen assistants. He stood at the left of Mister Roberts, flanking him with Doctor Githens.

"Ladies and gentlemen," Roberts began, to a wave of cheers that deafened the jeers. "We present the Incredible Machine."

All were silent, even those who watched out of anger rather than enthusiasm. All wished to look upon it, skeptics and otherwise, and no matter what the stated reason, they could not help but feel an anticipatory awe.

It emerged from the Laboratory upon that unfathomable rail, like a turtle's head poking from its shell. A quiet gasp rippled among the crowd. It was an awe-inspiring thing, this Incredible Machine, but somehow cruel looking. It was a great twisted confusion of pistons and levers and smokestacks. Already smoke

121

churned from its guts in great rumbling clouds—black smoke, green smoke, electric-blue smoke, smoke of a color that no one in the crowd could later quite agree on, that perhaps none had even seen before that day. Enormous, it seemed the size of several locomotives piled together, and in fact, in a way, could almost resemble that on the whole; not just piled together, but locomotives dissected, with every iron innard exposed, pulled painfully out, and twisted together in a confused, otherworldly tangle. From certain angles it almost seemed to *look* at an onlooker, although the illusion was only created by the haphazard mixture of machinery that made it up. And as the audience gazed upon it, it shuddered slightly as if slowly, steadily breathing. Later, many who were in the crowd that day would say they felt an odd chill shuddering down their spines as it screamed out on that rail; nothing joyous or excited, but instead, filled with an almost animal dread.

A scattershot applause rang out as the crowd shook off their initial reaction. The inventor stepped to the microphone, taking a last puff of his pipe.

"The Incredible Machine," Doctor Githens began simply. "Long have we been throwing our lives away to cross these vast seas. The ships which we have grown used to are clumsy things, apt to be lost in a storm or taken by pirates. But *not* the Incredible Machine. The Incredible Machine is made to cross utterly vast distances—the space between oceans—in the blink of an eye. It converts its matter into a separate dimension, in which all is much closer than it is here, before tearing out at a new point. We could take ourselves to China in a heartbeat. We could be in Antarctica in minutes. There is no obstacle that we cannot cross—perhaps, one day, we can take it to the heavens." He smiled, and the applause intensified.

"Although it's the former to which we'll be traveling first," the businesslike Roberts cut in with a roguish grin. He took the cigar out of his mouth (some swore you could hear the sound of it tearing from his lips) and stepped forward, crowding Githens away from the microphone. "Not quite built for Antarctic weather, and asides, I can barely fit a spare dogsled in there." A bark of forced laughter from certain sections of the crowd, a loud derisive boo from others. Mr. Roberts's face did not change. "On this day of wondrous inauguration, we will be traveling to China, where we have installed several loyal members of our crew waiting for our arrival." He did not mention the dozens of men who had been wasted upon the waters, sent out to reach this Chinese rendezvous, dashed to nothing upon the waves from whatever hell-storms brewed now in the Pacific. "We will send a telegram from that location before coming back to this very spot."

"If we have calculated this correctly," Githens added, not quite at the mic, "we should be disappearing from this very spot, and reappearing in the very same space within an hour."

Several *oohs* were heard. None had quite understood the mechanism of this great thing, this thing which rumbled before them and somehow hurt to look upon.

Joe was brought forward.

"Myself and the men of my union take pride in our work," he said curtly. "Don't fear for us." The crowd leaned forward, expecting more, but he shrank back from the microphone then, face unchanging.

After giving their last bows and waves, the three men disappeared into the machine.

Within, the machine was ever more confused, all made up of thousands upon thousands of endlessly interlocking tubes, gears and girders that made the head spin. The three men made their way through the labyrinthine tangles into the heart of the Incredible Machine.

Joe had spent many hours laboring to make the shell that encased the Machine's operating room, but he had not yet been permitted access to that central chamber. Classified, Githens had said, for only top men. And Joe had already felt a gnawing fear upon seeing a few of Githens' "top men," in very unscientific robes, who had been carving runes into the framework and chanting strange and confusing words that he couldn't make out over their handiwork. With such bizarre rituals in mind—which he had dismissively called *weird rich guy shit* in the pool hall—he felt a great acidic trepidation in his gut as the door to the control room opened.

This sense of vague fear was momentarily thwarted. This was a simple room. It was a dimly-lit room, mostly unadorned; just black iron and weak lamplight. Two chairs were bolted to the floor, one with a panel covered in glowing lights, keys, switches and levers. There was a long table, roughly the length and width of an adult man, with a pair of fetters at each end.

Joe looked at this table and the many levers and, for just a moment, wondered at their purpose. Then he felt a pinch at the back of his neck.

When he came to, he was shackled to the table.

Doctor Githens was fastening the last fetter around his wrist, waving his palsied hand in front of Joe's fluttering eyes.

"You do need to be awake for this," Githens said.

"Wha—," Joe began. He saw Roberts tossing an empty syringe into the trash receptacle.

"Steam is not going to get us across universes, my man," Doctor Githens said cheerfully. He had lowered himself into the chair closest to the control panel. Without a moment's pause he began to manipulate the levers, thin fingers smashing away at the keys.

Joe felt a humming that came from the console, that came from the fetters at his wrists and his ankles, from all around him, coursing through his body, setting him to shuddering.

Then, pain.

Pain spiderwebbing along his nerve endings, shooting out from his very bones. Pain wracked in every conceivable place where pain could be felt, like hot knives laid along his very core. He felt his stomach drop, felt strange, rhythmic vibrations of agony moving through him now.

The scholar threw another switch, stepped over to Joe. "Well?" he asked curtly.

Joe coughed, realized he'd been screaming.

"Githens?" he asked confusedly. He was lost in a haze of confused agony. "Please, sir. What happened. . . please."

"Were you hurt?"

"Oh yes, sir."

"Good. Pain is necessary." Githens took a note in his journal. "Looks like we have a rousing success, Mr. Roberts!"

"Hrrm," The executive grunted. He was reading a newspaper.

"What. . . " Joe coughed. "What are you doing to me?"

"Pain." Githens shook his head, clapping his hands together. "The Great Ones need pain, elsewise They will not let us cross the space between our universe's folds just. . . willy-nilly. It wants a soul, foremost, but a soul in agony is what it *really* needs. And we certainly need to travel further."

He threw the lever again, deftly operated more buttons. All the while, Joe felt as if he were exploding from inside. When it stopped, he coughed and sobbed.

"Please don't do this to me," he wept.

"Ahh, we *can't* be there yet," the scientist muttered as he bent over some figures.

"*Please.*" Joe was shrieking now. "Nothing could be worth this, no one should have to *feel* this. . . *please*, Githens, Roberts, *PLEASE*. . ."

Roberts shot him an irritated look. Githens simply shrugged to him as he made his way to the console.

"Will you kill me?" Joe asked in a final choked sob of despair.

"We must," the scholar answered. "Not immediately, but we must. You will be the great sacrifice that was made for this ultimate step. The bold man who was chosen to go where none had before, whole bravely offered himself up to fuel the most fantastic voyage of all. You will be an inspiration. The Man who Bought the Future. Your statues will adorn our City forevermore." And as Joe opened his mouth to make some final plaintive plea, Githens threw the switch.

Within a few minutes Joe was nearly dead. He was not cut open, his limbs were not broken; there was no blood whatsoever. And yet it could not possibly be ignored that his body had been drawn utterly to the bone, as if every ounce of intervening flesh had been drained dry then burned to nothing. The eyes gaped out of their sockets as if about to spill over, and the mouth lolled open with what was clearly a final death rattle; his body heaved and retched with the effort it took to draw a breath.

"*Fuck!*" Githens shouted.

The executive turned, irritated. "What now?"

"I don't think we're there," Githens muttered over his figures.

"Are you sure?" Roberts said curtly. "Can't we just, you know. . ." In lieu of a descriptive phrase, Roberts waved his hand at the clearly-dying Joe. "Do *that* a little more to him?"

"There's nothing left to take." Githens listened to Joe's chest with a stethoscope. "But we can at least have him look for us."

"Why don't you?" the executive snapped.

"If we're between worlds, it would utterly break the mind to look outside." Githens lowered a folding periscope from the shadowy ceiling. "I still have use for my mind. He doesn't."

Roberts gave a curt nod and reopened his newspaper. Githens started lowering the periscope to Joe's eye.

"I know that you must be fading fast," Githens said to the man who suffered so incredibly. "But please, look through this periscope, and to the best of the abilities that remain to you, describe what you see."

He lowered the lens over Joe's twitching eye, pinched his other eye shut, and waited.

There were a few moments of silence. Then, a choking noise; a small cracking noise. Something close to smoke was leaking from Joe's eye which was behind the lense. And then the screaming, hoarse and animalistic, worse than before. The wasted thing that had once been a factory worker writhed and screamed in a final pathetic death throe, before falling stiffly back on the table, that smoky substance now leaking from his eyes, nose, and ears.

"Well," Githens said darkly, "we are *certainly* not in China."

"So what are we to do, then, Githens?" Roberts asked impatiently.

"We can't go any farther without more fuel," Githens murmured, looking at the husk that lay before him.

"You don't want this to be a failure, do you?" Roberts said.

Githens said nothing. He was already pushing Joe off of the table, who slid to the floor with a dry thump. As dust from what was once Joe Peterson began to spiral up in the lamplight, Githens climbed onto the table.

"Do I need to shackle you?" Roberts asked.

"No," Githens said. "And the process is mostly automatic at this point. Just throw the red switch." Roberts began reaching for it before the scientist cut in with, "Wait."

"What," Roberts grunted impatiently.

"Put the shackles on me. And lower the periscope over my eye."

"Githens?"

"Do it!" the scientist barked. "Please, sir. It will be my only chance. A scientific marvel."

Roberts shrugged, shackled the scientist as requested, and lowered the periscope over his eye. And Githens felt a final sense of excitement rising as he pressed against the glass.

The sense did not last long.

The smoke was coming out of both eyes by the time Githens could scream coherently. "Please!" he shrieked. "Get it away from me! Take the periscope away! *I don't want to see!*"

Roberts thought about complying, but he was already sitting, already buckled in. And he *could* reach the red switch from where he sat.

So he threw it.

Roberts, never a creative man, lacked the language to describe the sounds that the scientist made as they traveled on. He watched as the already sickly-looking man was drained utterly, watched the skin draw right to the bone, watched the one visible eye bursting from the socket, steamlike substance pouring from every orifice in his head. While it was not something which the executive's cold lizard-brain could really be actively aware of, there was a part of him that noticed how the scholar's screams never sounded like they were in pain, but instead, seemed to be ever-intensifying screams of horror at the truths he looked upon through that periscope.

The Incredible Machine

Finally the Machine stopped shaking. Roberts stood, and towered over the scientist as he lay twitching and dying on the table.

"Are we in China?" Roberts asked curtly.

It took a moment for Githens to do anything, but, incredibly, almost imperceptibly, he nodded as he died.

Winston Roberts grinned as he ascended the tight corridors of the Incredible Machine. His grin widened as he threw open the heavy iron door to the outside. And he was positively aglow by the time he stepped out into the fading daylight, raising his hands to the wild cheers of a gathered crowd.

About the Author

When not writing surreal horror, sci-fi, and fantasy, Dennis Conrad performs bad stand-up comedy to a captive audience—in other words, he teaches English to high schoolers. A native of the Philadelphia area, Dennis spends too much of his time reading, watching, and otherwise consuming the kind of weird dark works that he also loves writing.

*****~~~~*****

Stockholm, 2066

by Joseph Sidari

"Your Majesties, Your Royal Highnesses, Your Excellencies, Ladies and Gentlem—"

A burst of feedback whined, and I reacted instinctively to cover my ears. My silver-gloved hands bounced off the bubble-style helmet on my head. From my spot on the podium I looked around, searching for the source of the noise. I tapped twice on the small, black box atop the lectern, and the screeching faded. A few strands of my graying hair drooped over my eyes. I flicked my head from side to side to clear my view, so I could read the foolish teleprompter and fulfill a friend's dying request. A head-to-toe environmental suit was not the outfit I'd have chosen for this—but hey, survivors can't be choosers. Right?

I forced a smile. This was for posterity. I should do my best to look happy—not terminal. I gripped the edges of the antique, oaken lectern before me, as if the thing might gallop off the otherwise barren stage, and tried to keep my voice steady.

"This year is an historic one for the Nobel Foundation—in so many ways. To begin with, this is the first time in over a hundred years, when Dr. Linus Pauling, was honored twice for his work in chemistry and nuclear disarmament, that previous Nobel laureates are being awarded The Prize again."

(PAUSE, AND WAIT FOR APPLAUSE TO DIE DOWN)

I read the teleprompter and then scanned the empty auditorium, not sure whether to laugh or cry. The overhead fluorescent lights hummed above my head in the Stockholm Concert Hall. Hoo-boy. Someone has a black sense of humor. The applause has all died—that's for sure. I let out the breath I'd been holding and continued. For Henrik.

"Almost 400 years ago, Sir Isaac Newton said, 'If I have seen further, it is by standing on the shoulders of giants.' This year's recipients would certainly agree with that statement. Over the centuries, many have studied infectious disease. Those ground-breaking men and women pulled medicine out of the dark ages, discovering that many ailments were caused by microscopic organisms—bacteria—and not by evil spirits or poor moral character. But it was not until the close of the 19th century that Louis Pasteur identified particles that were even smaller than a bacterium. Thus, the field of virology was born."

My cheeks flushed. Sweat dripped from my shoulder blades, and down the small of my back. If I didn't know better, I'd say I was coming down with something. Ha! If only. But maybe—just maybe—the latest concoction they injected into me is actually doing something. I relaxed my grip on the lectern and lifted a hand to fiddle with the controls on my environmental suit. Several lines of glowing red text popped up inside my faceplate. Tapping at another button on the suit, the data morphed from red to green. I cleared my throat, ignored

132

the perspiration, and focused my gaze back at the camera and prompter.

"Past recipients have won The Prize for their work in diabetes. Heart disease. Cancer. But the two individuals we honor today had set their sights on a humbler target: the common cold.

"Many refer to the common cold as if it is one entity. It is not. Like the flu, it is made of many different viral strains. Modern medicine has developed treatments for other viral illnesses—using drugs from acyclovir to zidovudine. But until recently, our best weapons against the cold were still based on folk wisdom. Drink fluids. Get rest. Take vitamin C.

"Since the cold virus is constantly changing and adapting, an effective treatment must do likewise. Unfortunately none could. That is, until virologist, Dr. Ji Sun Pan, collaborated with nanoscience engineer, Dr. Patricia Doran.

"They met by chance in a pharmacy—both were scheduled to speak at a symposium on global health. Doran was getting a decongestant for her sinus headache, and Pan was purchasing cough drops. In their mutual respiratory misery, they decided to put their degrees together and solve this common problem.

"They knew it would be necessary for their new antiviral therapy to be smart. It must learn fast and adapt faster. But it should also be cheap. Health care innovation is not just for the first world, but for the whole world. The timing was just right. Nanotech could now create an artificially intelligent targeting system that could be piggy-backed onto an airborne vector created in the virology lab. In doing this, they created the first robot you could spray up your nose. Once there, their creation could alter and adapt, attacking whatever version of the cold virus was present, and rid our bodies from this age-old scourge.

"This Pan-Doran Vaccine was nicknamed FiDO, standing for Final Disease Obliteration. But FiDO was also the perfect nickname for mankind's new best friend, right? And the public was clamoring for it. That is why the Americans and their FDA rushed FiDO though Phase One, Phase Two, and eventually Phase Three trials. At first it only had limited availability in the U.S. as a nasal spray. But as word spread of its success against the cold virus, the other peoples of the world were clamoring to get FiDO, too. Under extreme public pressure, the World Health Organization relented, and stated FiDO was *probably safe enough* for greater distribution. The nasal inhaler was discarded in favor of an aerosol that could be sprayed into the air. And then it was carried by the wind—from city to town to village—to be breathed in by all of humanity.

"FiDO was a smart one, all right. It quickly learned how to neutralize not just the various iterations of the cold virus, but any virus. It targeted and eradicated previously incurable infections like HIV. Ebola. And the coronavirus, with all its lovely mutations.

"Ooh. . . what the—?" I grimaced, and then reached down to grab my belly. My intestines rumbled, gurgled. Vesuvius ready to erupt. I tapped a button on my suit and more red glowing data projected on my inside face shield. I manipulated the buttons of my environmental suit a few times and the data glowed green again. I dropped my hand back down to check my abdomen. No eruption today. Too bad. I had thought we were onto something.

"Every viral illness was soon hunted to extinction. And then FiDO did something neither Pan nor Doran anticipated: it altered its programming to seek out something new. Something *not* a virus. With sniper-like efficiency, this wonder drug set its sights on the virus-*like* particles known as prions. And before you could say 'Mad Cow Disease,' the Creutzfeld–Jakob particle was dead and

134

buried. Score another win for FiDO. But as we all know this tenacious little pup was just getting started.

"One by one, pathogen after pathogen was seized tightly and shaken to death in FiDO's iron jaw grip, until only the lowly bacterial infections remained. Not to worry, though. These efficient little nanobots had a built-in desire to serve their master. From strep throat to venereal disease, FiDO identified and eliminated them all. Within a year, humanity enjoyed a health it had never known since Adam and Eve first shared their germs biting into the same apple.

"But this is old news—cribbed from a speech by my predecessor—God rest his soul. It was delivered when Drs. Pan and Doran were awarded their first Nobel Prize for Medicine in 2049. But it is critical for me to restate these details, for they are the reasons why these two *brilliant* researchers are now being awarded. . ." I blinked away a tear. "Awarded the Nobel Prize for Peace."

That tear tracked down my cheek. I swiped at it, but my gloved hand bounced off my helmet's face shield again. "No!" I slammed down my gloved hand on the lectern, and then shook my head.

"Recording this speech for the Nobel archives seems like one of the most useless things I have done in my long history with this venerable organization." Sorry, Henrik. A promise is a promise, but I must do this my own way. I cleared my throat.

"Apologies to Your Majesty." I bowed to an empty spot on the stage. "And to you, too, old friend. All that stuff I just said, well, it is a lie. Look at me: I'm the Emperor Nero. Rome has burnt to the ground, and I'm holding my fiddle in one hand and this canned speech about world peace in the other. If my words are to have any meaning, I'd better tell them to you straight." A lock of hair dropped before my eyes again, but I was not reading the script anymore, so I ignored it.

"Yes—we are currently at peace now. Why, you may ask? Because we are disease-free? Because we decided to beat our swords into vaccines? No. I don't think so. I'd like to say for the record that I did not want to award these two *giants of science* the Peace Prize, but it was my director's last wish. No other prizes are going to be awarded this year. Or possibly any year. Ever. Henrik desired that we should present this last ever Nobel Prize to the architects of our current state. And since he knew he would not live to do it himself, he made me swear to do so." I turned my eyes heavenward.

"Henrik, I hope this makes you happy. Do you mind if I digress for a moment, my mentor? My old friend? I'd like to tell a little story about my childhood in Oslo." I paused, and scanned the auditorium.

"Well, I suppose since there's no one here to object—no men, no women, not even Henrik's ghost is here to tell me to shut up and finish—I will proceed. But first a little about me. And my father.

"Harold Anderson was a big blonde bear of a man. 'Strong as an ox and twice as smart,' he used to brag. Well, he would go hunting for elk in the mountains, up north, in Buskerud County. I cried each time he bundled up in his camouflaged parka, angry at him for killing those beautiful animals. He would pat my head and laugh, saying, 'Heidi, one day you will understand. One day you might even join me.'

"'Never-never-never' I cried. I would never understand why he was so mean-spirited. One time, when I was a teen and carrying on about his cruelty, I tried to explain to me about animal conservation. He said that with few natural predators, if the hunters did not periodically thin the herd each winter, there would not be enough food for all the elk. And if that were so, then ten times the number of animals that were hunted would eventually starve and die. A harsh fact I had a hard time wrapping my teenaged brain around. I think at the time I sulked and mumbled that he should go out and plant more elk food instead of slaughtering the helpless creatures.

"Well, now I do understand. The infectious diseases that had hunted humanity were now extinct. They were no longer thinning our herd, and the human population exploded. Soon we outstripped our food supply. And since no one ever planted more 'elk food' for us, all those healthy humans across the planet started dying of starvation—by the millions.

"But wait. We're forgetting about something, aren't we? Remember FiDO? What did that bored, yet oh-so-clever doggie do during all of this? Could man's best friend change yet again? Of course it could—but not in a way that humanity would like.

"What do you do for an encore when you have wiped out every microscopic plague and pestilence in human history? You know the answer: you look for another target. That's when it began killing the bacteria on our skin. And in our GI tract. Bacteria that were critical for our human homeostasis—and that of our planet. No job is too big for our little FiDO, though. In no time, this efficient nanobot made short work of all the bacteria in our body—and on our world. Every—"

I bit off the words with distaste— "Last. One."

"You know the rest. If you were lucky enough to have stockpiled some food during the overpopulation phase, you could no longer digest it without bacteria in your gut. Taking probiotics didn't help—FiDO was in the air, in our water—everywhere. It took care of those new microbes as soon as they entered our system. The diarrhea, malnutrition, and dehydration afterwards made folks pray for the days of salmonella and dysentery. The only way to survive was synthetic TPN—total parenteral nutrition. If you thought safe food and clean water were a scarce resource before, readily absorbable intravenous amino acids and carbohydrates were even more so. Available to only a few in the most technologically advanced and privileged countries. Like here. And like me. And even in those places, 99% of the population was wiped out before IV foodstuffs could be mass-produced.

"Then, for an encore, FiDO altered its programming yet again. After all, why just go after bacteria in the humans? It attacked the bacteria colonizing the birds in the sky." I wave my hands at the roof over the hall. Then the fish in the sea. . . "

I slammed both fists on the lectern. "FiDO eventually exterminated the bacteria in any and all creatures that moved on God's *formerly* green Earth."

I am ranting. I need to calm down. To finish. I held my breath and counted to five. I felt no better, but I could try to speak without sounding like a crazy woman—at least I hoped so.

"And then there was none. Dead bodies. Everywhere. And with no bacteria to let them decay, to release nitrogen into the soil, the plants died. And without plants carrying out photosynthesis, our atmosphere became starved for oxygen. And that's why I wear this."

I pointed to my shiny silver environmental suit.

"I have oxygen to breathe. Nutrition injected into my veins. And mummified dead bodies surrounding me, outside this hall, stacked like cordwood in preparation for the long Swedish winter.

"So now we have *peace*. And *health*. Thanks to the Pan-Doran Vaccine that was loosed upon the world. There are other researchers—who are still alive. Perhaps they are not so *brilliant* as Pan and Doran, as they try to develop a synthetic bacteria, yeast, or virus that can take up residency in our ecosystem. To restore balance. That is the other reason for my environmental suit. I have been injected with some new synthetic bacteria three times now. I hope to God this most recent strain will survive. It feels like there is a battle going on inside me. I'm not sure who is winning, but I worry it's FiDO.

"You see, we have since learned that FiDO has inserted itself into our bone marrow. My bone marrow. It has mutated, replicated and then killed off every foreign bacteria-like substance that we have been able to create so far. I suspect it's too late for us—hence the current planet-wide quarantine. No one can travel to the space stations, or the moon base. And especially not the Martian colonies. Let's hope that bad doggie Pan and Doran created can't cross the vacuum of space and get to Mars." I shuddered.

"But maybe, just maybe a breakthrough will happen, and humanity will survive here. On Earth. Where it all began. We can't lose hope, right?

"Until then, we lucky survivors will need to remember how we got here at this time and place in history. And hope that maybe someone will find a cure for the Pan-Doran vaccine, and our hubris. Therein lies the reason for this recording. Now, where was I? Oh yes." I giggled. "The presentation of The Prize.

"All right Henrik, I'm wrapping up." I cleared my throat, speaking now in the proper and ceremonial manner that befitted this solemn occasion. "On behalf of the Nobel Assembly at Karolinska Institutet, I wish to convey, posthumously, to the esteemed Dr. Ji Sun Pan and Dr. Patricia Doran our . . ."

I hesitated, not sure how to say the next two words. I spat them out, like poison. "*Our congratulations. The good doctors died six and eight months ago, respectively, but my speech will ensure that all of humanity will remember them. And revile them. They are the ones responsible for *this*. This peace we now enjoy. Traditionally the recipients, or their representatives, would accept The Prize from the hand of the King. But after multiple calls to each university, I have learned that not one of their colleagues remain alive to accept it on their behalf, and—" I bowed my head in respect, "—His Majesty, the King of Sweden. . . well, he died last month."

I reached down below the lectern and grabbed the prop I had placed there earlier, to finish off my speech. I raised an antique, Orrefors wine glass into the air. "May whatever God that looks over our pathetic planet, the God who demonstrated wisdom in letting us get sick and then get better. To fall ill and sometimes die. May that God spare future generations from any more of this kind of health and peace. *Skol!*" I pantomimed a drink, and then threw the glass from the stage where it shattered into a thousand crystal shards on the concert hall floor.

"And may God take mercy on our oh-so-healthy souls."

About the Author

Joseph Sidari (www.josephsidari.com) writes from outside of Boston. Some of his prior works were published in the Third Flatiron anthology, *Monstrosities*, and Emerald Bay Books' anthology, *Horror for Hire: Second Shift,* and also online in *The Arcanist*, and *Daily Science Fiction*, among others.

*****~~~~*****

All Your Bases, Yada-Yada

by Paula Hammond

It doesn't matter what time or day I take the train, they're always there.

Today, the faded beauty in fake fur eating cheese squares is on her own. Sometimes she's paired with a rock dude. All death-skull rings and bad tattoos.

We must be about to hit Kings Cross, because the passenger alarm in the loo goes off, and the lady eating grapes out of the Fenman's paper bag rolls her eyes at me tiredly. Last time she was eating cherries and was sat with a rumpled guy doing *The Times* crossword. They fussed together like married couples do, she tucking down the label in the back of his shirt, he picking lint off her coat. Today, they're strangers. She sits in an aisle seat, but he's still stuck on the anagram.

As I leave the train, the guy with the food trolly clips my ankle. He's so busy playing with his phone, he doesn't notice, even when I give him my best Paddington Bear stare. One day I'm going to throw him off train and see if he notices that.

The tube is busy, but not so busy that I don't recognize the young Russian hogging three seats with his tool bags, as he always does.

The Cockney geezers at the curb-side garage wolf-whistle as I walk past. Just like they do everyday. I've given up being embarrassed.

On the corner, I inevitably bump into the wizened Chinese lady—two smears of rouge on each cheek, tiny eyebrows painted high on her forehead like rogue m-dashes. She's so small she wears children's clothes, and, today, she's dressed in an implausible combination of Thomas the Tank T-shirt and pink combat trousers. At least that shows some imagination, though the fact that I see her absolutely everywhere is not only ridiculous, it's plain lazy. Whoever's responsible for this part of reality really needs to up their game.

Plus, there are simply too many Grahams. It's a popular name, sure, but I know at least twenty. And they're all variations on a theme. Ginger, freckled, geeky. I'm betting the programmer is called Graham. Like I said: lazy.

What keeps me awake at night isn't the knowledge that I live in a simulacrum. What makes my brain itch are the same questions that bug all sentient beings. What's it all about? Where do I fit into the scheme of things?

Even if all this were real, I'd have the same questions, so I guess it doesn't really matter. Life's one big puzzle. And death? Is death a sham too? Maybe the real me is plugged into some all-singing, all-dancing virtual reality. When I get to Game Over, perhaps I'll just un-plug and go walk the dog. That's comforting, at least.

I've accepted that I may never know the truth, but I've always hoped that, one day, someone will slip up and I'll get to peer behind the curtains. See the face of God. Or the Head Programmer. Which may be one and the same. That's a less comforting thought, to be honest. I'm not sure

I like the idea of IT Graham—all prepubescent sweat glands and wandering hands—pushing my buttons.

Still, I think that's why I spotted it. Because I've always been looking for it.

It was a small thing. A handful of missing pixels is the best way to describe it. A backlit nothing that drew the eye. I wouldn't have noticed it at all, if I hadn't chosen to walk home past the old railway bridge. At least I think I made the choice. Maybe IT Graham was messing with my head.

I decided not to get into too much of a knot about the who's and why's. The fact was, I finally had proof. I poked at it. Got a nice electric shock for my troubles, and, while it was fizzing like a fly trapped in a strip-light, the whole railway arch shimmered. I've played enough computer games to know a glitch when I see one, so I decided to push it.

I dug out my ubiquitous, city-commuter, re-usable water bottle and poured the contents onto my hands. I slapped my hands over the missing pixels and waited. For a moment nothing happened. I don't know what I was expecting, I simply figured; computers, electricity, not a good mix. Then, suddenly, there was an enormous whoosh, and I was thrown six foot across the gravel track. I landed hard enough to knock myself out and came to with my fillings aching and my nostrils full of the scent of singed hair. Mine.

For a second I thought it was night, but this is London. It's never really dark. There's always the glow of the city, squatting like some radioactive lizard on the horizon.

This was can't-see-a-hand-in-front-of-your-face levels of dark. I toyed with the idea that my body had vanished, along with everything else, and now I was some disembodied consciousness. A genuine ghost in the machine. Then, I fell over my own feet and had to concede it seemed unlikely.

143

If I put out a hand, I found I could follow the route of the railway bridge by the weird tingling sensation I got when my fingers brushed against the nothing. I counted steps until I came to Boundary Road—as solid and as perfectly rendered as ever—then I stepped from the big-empty back into the world.

I turned around and retraced my steps to the site of the missing pixels. I couldn't see a damn thing of course, but at one point, I heard singing. An actual, full-on shower ballad.

Gingerly, I felt my way to the spot I'd drenched ten minutes ago—ready for the kick. Instead of a jolt, all I got was blancmange. A tacky spot that my hand seemed to sink into.

I figured, why not? I pushed as hard as I could, and the spot started to give. Slowly at first, then, all at once, I was up to my elbow in ethereal jelly. What was unnerving was that I could still feel my hand, and, wherever it was, it was raining. Hard, gritty summer rain and, with it, came the synesthetic impression of a city, heavy with pollution and the press of humanity.

So, okay, I freaked. I pulled my hand out and hyperventilated until my face went numb. Then I hunkered on my haunches, pulled my shit together, and came up with a plan.

I jogged home and retrieved my wireless bike-cam. I wound a ball of twine around the circumference until it was about the size of a tennis ball then headed back to the void. I found my sticky little oubliette and lodged my camera-ball half-way in. I wasn't sure I'd get a signal unless some of the camera was here, in my world.

I was shaking by the time I got back home. I locked the doors, poured myself a stiff whisky—the expensive stuff I save for birthdays—sat down, and switched on. I was so fazed that I punched in the wrong password. I tried again. Failed again. Terrified I'd lock myself out, I took a deep breath and input the numbers as slowly as I could. Bingo!

I opened the cycle app and saw nothing beyond static. No—wait—not static. Rain. The little camera seemed to be against the wall of a house. Above, a blocked drain was vomiting out muddy water, nesting materials, and bird poop. But it was there! Wherever there was.

I had maybe an hour of battery life left, unless the rain killed the camera, which seemed likely given the downpour. I sat and finished the bottle, eyes glued to the screen, before quietly passing out.

I woke up, drool-face glued to the table top, head thumping. But that wasn't going to stop me. I rinsed my head under the tap and headed out, practically buzzing with excitement.

Usually, when you cross Boundary Road, you hit Rosebank. On the corner there's an odd Swiss Cottage sort of building, nestled under the railway bridge. Follow Boundary east, and you hit the High Street. Walk down Rosebank, and you're quickly into rows of light industrial units nestled under the arches. Last night, Rosebank had been in blackout. Now, it didn't exist at all. And, just to add to that lurching feeling of dislocation, the Swiss Cottage was a garage. The one that had always been two streets down, where the Cockney geezers practiced their cheesy patter on every woman between the ages of sixteen and sixty.

I tramped back home, deflated, and fired up the bike cam app. Over a quadruple espresso I went through each rainy, grainy frame. Before the camera gave out, a figure walked right up and peered at the lens. She wriggled her nose in a way that was eerily familiar, gave the lens an experimental poke, smiled, and turned to walk away. The last frame was a back view—red curls imprisoned by a silver clip in the shape of a wolf. The same one was on my bedside table, only my hair wasn't long enough to wear it anymore. This other me clearly hadn't had her annual Summer shearing yet.

It was while I was digesting that particular mind-fuck that I noticed something. Right in the corner of the screen: GPS coordinates.

I clicked on the coordinates, and a map materialized.

Now, ask a lot of born-and-bred Londoners where they're from and they'll say Hackney, Clapham, Wanstead—one of the boroughs. I know Londoners who've never even been on the tube and certainly never go into 'the City'. Me? I've breathed in every inch of this big, nasty, beautiful metropolis, and I know it in a way that only someone who grew up in a claustrophobic Scots village, in the arse-end of nowhere, can. So I knew there was no way the map could be right.

I bolted down some toast, worked out a safe-ish cycle route, and headed off.

It took half an hour of serious pedaling and the same again of backtracking down alley-ways to find it. The road headed uphill towards Old Street, but if I screwed up my eyes, there was a sort of heat-haze and, in it, another road with a Swiss Cottage on the corner. I followed the ghost road, working hard to ignore the screaming voice in my head that told me I was going to die in some bone-crunching traffic accident.

My body hit the haze. The sensation was so unsettling that I immediately fell off the bike. I was still picking the gravel out of my bloodied knees when a petite woman with a serious resting bitch-face hauled me up and motioned me to follow her.

She led me back to her—our—house and helped me patch up the cuts. "So," she asked, looking me up and down in that judgmental way I have too, "who the hell are you supposed to be?"

"I could ask you the same thing," I said defensively.

"That camera was yours?"

I nodded.

"You know, I did the exact same thing? Couple of months back. But it wasn't you on my camera, was it? No glasses." She gestured vaguely.

"Huh. What did you see?"

"A beach."

"Nice. Always wanted to live by the sea."

"Yeah. Me too."

"You haven't been there?"

"Not yet. I was reluctant to buy any deeper into this 'I'm living in the Matrix' shizz. Didn't seem healthy."

She wasn't quite my double. Close. But there were enough differences to notice.

"So, what do you think?"

"Multiple versions of the same reality, all a bit different, like someone's trying out story branches of a sim-game."

"Do you think we're the only ones who are. . . aware?"

"Is it all about me? Damned if I know."

"What do you want to do?" I asked.

"Nothing. Real or not, my life's not so bad that I'm rushing towards the alternative."

"Which is?"

"Oblivion. Can't see how it would end any other way."

I gave her a hard stare, and she returned it with a sort of exhausted resignation.

"I can't live like this," I said. "Knowing someone's out there, playing games, pulling strings."

She shrugged. "You do you. It's not like I'm going to brain you with an iron skillet and bury you in the garden. Did think about it, tho," she added without a shred of irony.

Next day, I headed out to work an hour earlier. Despite that, all the usual suspects were there, so I started small. Plonked myself down next to anagram guy and gave him the solution. For a micro-moment he froze. Actually froze. Then, he pouted passive-aggressively and put down his paper. I swooped past fruit lady, whisked the bag out of her hand and dumped a chocolate bar in it. She blinked, did an odd little judder then started to eat as though nothing had happened. I headed for the loo, locked myself in and sat there until the train stopped. For the first time in forever the alarm didn't go off. As I left, I spotted trolly dude, grabbed his cart, and rammed it into him as hard as I could. This time the trolly actually shimmered before 'reality' clicked back in, and he began swearing and nursing his bruised shins.

I continued in wrecking-ball mode all the way home. I threw the Russian's tools off the seat and sat next to him, adopting my best man-spreading posture. The Cockney geezers were easy meat. I walked straight up to the short one and told him I was "waiting for my order of sexist bullshit." Shorty fritzed, his mouth opening and closing wordlessly as he shuffled back and forth in a repeating loop. When I left him, he was still doing it.

The Chinese lady was trickier. I figured all that walking around must be exhausting, so I invited her home. Gāo Mingmei seemed like a sweet thing, but her eyes were dead. For the first ten minutes it was like talking to one of those AI live-chat assistants. It was when IT Graham came online that things got interesting.

"Give it up, Maggie. You know it won't end well."

"What?" I stared at the little Chinese lady. Her eyes flickered, and, for the first time, she looked at me—really looked at me.

"Graham?"

"What?" Confusion. Then hollow laughter. "Oh, you think you're so clever."

"Do I? You tell me?"

"What I'll tell you is this," Mingmei, leaned forward, her mouth twisting in an ugly snarl, "stop fucking with my programme, or I'll delete your fucking ass."

"Oh?" My stomach gave a traitorous flip, but I tried to keep my tone even. "Why don't you do that then?"

"What?" Mingmei shook her head. "Oh! No! That's just sad. You do, don't you? You think you're an actual player character? Shall I tell you what you are? Nothing. That's what. A bit of faulty programming with delusions of grandeur."

I tried to ignore the fact that what she said sounded horribly plausible. "So, why haven't you already deleted me?"

"Because you're funny, bitch!" Mingmei was inches away from me now, sneering, jabbing those perfect little fingers in my face. "Look at me! I'm so special. Watching you trying to work it all out. . . Priceless!"

Despite all the 'clues,' I'd never believed 100 percent that my world was a fake. It was a joke, that became a nagging suspicion, that became something that made me queasy if I thought about it too much. Because only crazy people really believe stuff like that. But, you know, crazy or not, sometimes you just have to commit.

I leant over, grabbed Mingmei's tiny head, and twisted. There was a crunch, a pop. She looked at me wide-eyed, lips turning blue, gulping for air like a fish out of water. I let go, and she toppled towards the floor, landing with barely a sound—she was so very, very small. Those raised, painted eyebrows made her look surprised. Yeah, well, I guess she wasn't expecting that.

I sat down with a thump, looked at the corpse on my kitchen floor, and started shaking. Then I started laughing, like the homicidal maniac I so clearly was. Oh, God! What the hell had I done?

I was still laughing hysterically, when everything went dark. Only it wasn't like the railway arches. This time there really was nothing. No room, no floor, no fingers, no toes.

I don't know how long I stood there, if stand is a word you can use when you don't have a body. I was giggling, choking, close to losing it for good, when, with a flicker, everything was back to normal. No Mingmei, and, outside, it was morning.

It was all too much. My heart was pounding. I could barely breathe. I needed air. I flung open the door, and there she was. All outdoorsy, wind-burnt, and pig-tails. She pushed past, heading for the kitchen. I followed, reeling.

"Fecker tried to wipe me," she said in a broad Irish brogue.

"Me too," I replied, in a sick, quiet whisper.

"Yeah. That's why I'm here." She pointed vaguely behind me at a little camera lodged, unnoticed, in the brickwork beside the fridge.

"Didn't bloody work tho, did it?" She grinned, and instantly all my doubts and fears evaporated. Her glee was infectious. It was part of me too, after all.

"What are you going to do?"

"All your bases are belong to us, yada-yada," she laughed. "Well, don't just stand there, I'm dying for a cuppa, and we can't plan a war without tea."

I preferred coffee myself, but it's those little differences that makes us what we are, right?

About the Author

Paula Hammond is a professional writer based in London. She reads too much and sleeps too little.

*****~~~~~*****

Kwatt Games

by Alyce Campbell

First Contact

A rare black stormy night broken by stabs of forked lightning. Hunched over the wheel of her truck, Sheriff Amelia Largo bounced along the rain-battered gravel road, tensely watching for soft muddy spots that trapped tires, as heavy thunderclaps rattled the truck.

Abruptly the thin beams from her headlights were swamped by dazzling brightness from an amber ring hovering over the creosote bush scrub not ten feet away. Gears groaned as her foot crushed the brake pedal. The engine stalled, and she thought she had popped the clutch, so she tried the ignition. Just a clink-clink-clink. "Shoot! Dead battery?" she muttered.

With a deep sigh, Amelia zipped up her slicker and climbed out of the pickup to confront the lights. She made a mental note to file a complaint. She was getting tired of bumping into the failed experiments of the crazy astro-engineers and flyboys from Area 51.

As she rounded the truck, the amber lights flickered then turned an extreme and painful yellow, illuminating what looked like a tormented golf cart trundling towards her. The strange conveyance halted about two yards away. An ill-defined gray shape leaned out one side and pointed a square object at her. Electric shocks jolted her chest and she fell, paralyzed. As her face scraped against rocks, the lights faded. . .

Stabbing pain in her left earlobe provoked her awake. She found herself almost buried in a body-hugging, toadstool-shaped gray chair, facing a toadstool-shaped gray desk. Definitely not standard. . . or even hush-hush. . . military issue. Neither seeing nor sensing any restraints, she tried to stand. Her legs wouldn't or couldn't respond. But she did succeed in raising her hand to her aching ear. A metallic strip about the width and length of a small staple chilled her finger.

Gray doors straight out of space opera slid open, and a gray something about her height but a body shaped like a giant cigar shuffled in. The something sat down across the desk from her, saturating the air with the smell of garlic. Oversized obsidian ovals lacking pupils fixed on her face. She eyeballed back and decided the gray exterior was an envirosuit, the obsidian ovals eye protectors resembling swimmers' goggles.

Lips tight, jaw clenched, Amelia determined to wait her captor out, to force him. . . or her. . . or whatever. . . to make the first move. After a protracted and silent staring contest, the gray-clad creature whistled and chirped, exciting the metal strip to life, revealing its purpose: translating.

The translating was far from perfect. After several stuttering stumbles, the translator settled into a deadpan baritone and produced phrases that were barely intelligible.

"Kwatt I, top boss of this scout flying object. Take you a must regrettable."

Aliens? Aliens! Not a flyboy prank! She gulped but replied as if this meeting was workaday. "I am Amelia."

"Amelia. . . your land boat regrettable."

152

She guessed the creature was apologizing for stopping her truck.

"Okay, apology accepted. Kwatt, why are you here?"

"Planet rich in you call oxidane. We want."

Amelia rummaged through disjointed fragments of her college chemistry class. "You mean water. You want to buy water."

Salvos of grating chirps were followed by a gap while the translator struggled. At last, "Ha, ha! Joke! We give prized stuffs for oxidane? No! No! I send tweet, many UFOs come, clean up rocky orb, take."

Another gap. "One rule. No taken from orbs with smart life. Find leader, we must, and test."

Amelia paled. *'Clean up'* could only mean many dreadful acts leading to the most dreadful of all. . . human extermination. She decided as sheriff of the county she could claim to be the leader.

"How considerate of you. Well smart life needs water too. And you're in luck. I'm the leader around here. What is your test?"

"Three puzzles. Solve you, we go different place. Maybe little orb clutched by giant six gas orb. Much harder to take. No dry place. Cold."

"Ah. . . Enceladus. Moon of Saturn."

"Said I so."

Amelia hoped alien and human thinking were similar, or the puzzles would be hopelessly foreign and ungraspable.

"First puzzle. Thing always 1 to 6; always 15 to 20; always 5. Only 21 if flying."

"Kind of long. Can I write the words down?"

"No, but I repeat," and the creature did.

Amelia focused and thought about all kinds of ratios. Her mind drifted to odds, calling to mind Las Vegas. A eureka moment!

153

"Dice! You mean dice. Six-sided objects for playing games."

"Ha, ha! Joke! Yes. . . long boredoms in scout UFO. Games, we play much."

The garlic reek intensified.

Amelia managed a small empathetic-sounding chuckle, worried what they gambled with. . . and for.

"Second puzzle. On scout UFO, we hold much fierce WockerJabber in cage which grows double each earth rotate, if we feed lots. If creature eats lots, in ten rotates it fill cage. How many rotates to fill quarter of cage and half of cage?"

Inwardly scowling, Amelia flashed back to memories of tedious logic puzzles that delighted her math professors. The most tedious was Froggy in the Well, solved by thinking backwards. WockerJabber must be half-sized at nine days, so would be quarter sized on the eighth day.

She smiled. "Half at nine, quarter at eight."

"Ha, ha, ha! Joke! Joke! So you do arithmetic. Now puzzle third."

Kwatt half-turned and flapped what might have been a limb. Three doors in three different shades of gray emerged from the wall.

"Door one go to engine. Toss you in, you fry. Door two go to oxidane holder. Toss you in, you drown. Door three go to WockerJabber, starved many rotates. Toss you in, you WockerJabber snack. Choose door."

For a few seconds, Amelia squeezed down vomit. She was about to lose, and her loss would doom humankind. Then she squared her shoulders, swallowed hard, and took a deep breath. Better to die with head held high. She glared at the creature. Her first step: protest that this puzzle was no puzzle at all, just an unfair trick. Before she could speak, he repeated, "Choose door." She wondered if he had a face and if the face was locked in a smirk.

154

Smirks! Gamblers and tells and bluffs! She shouted, "Three. . . I choose door three."

Piercing chirps and ear-splitting trills swirled around fast and furious, and the garlic stench approached intolerable. The translator delivered strings of words liberally salted with vulgar oaths and damnations.

Door three slid open and revealed what Amelia had expected, based on the second puzzle: an alien animaloid cowering in a corner. Under two feet tall and scrawny, the animaloid appeared half-dead. Amelia felt pity, until it snarled and bared pointy brown-stained teeth.

The translator struggled, searching for the right words. "Too smarty pants leader. You go now. We go now."

Coming to, Amelia found herself stretched out on the wet road beside her truck. Storm over, the sky an inky velvet expanse teeming with diamonds. She sat up, using the front wheel as a pillow, and thought muddy rubber never smelled so wonderful. As the circle of amber lights rose vertically and disappeared into the blackness, a strong "good riddance" formed on her lips.

. . .

Second Contact

Another long day manning the Sheriff's office. Another rough ride home on a moonless night. Amelia Largo, her teeth grinding each time the old pickup hit a rut or a ridge in the winding road, was looking forward to a late-evening meal of reheated tuna casserole washed down with hot coffee. As she bounced along, she tried to build a case strong enough to convince the county administrator to spend some money on a new truck so she could hunt for criminals in greater comfort. The replacement didn't need to be fresh off the assembly line. Just newer. Just less beat up—with better shock absorbers.

The night was broken by a circle of yellow lights, hovering a foot above the gravel about three car lengths ahead. She flattened the brake pedal. The engine whined.

Died. Amelia jumped out of the truck, ready to read the riot act to whoever was flying drones so darn near the road. She had stomped only a few feet when something spiked hit her shoulder. She flopped nose first into a patch of weeds.

When she came to, a familiar garlic-reeking alien sat across from her behind a familiar gray desk. Her ear lobe throbbed again from being squeezed by the alien's translator device.

With zero enthusiasm, Amelia said, "Hello Kwatt. What brings you back to the neighborhood?"

This time the alien did not apologize for stopping her truck. "Ha. . . ha. . . ha. . . so you memory good for faces."

Amelia wrinkled her nose and sighed. "Well, to be precise, I have never seen your face—only the bling envirosuit and goofy goggles you're wearing. But you are hard to forget."

"You not so easy for Kwatt to memory. All runts on this orb look same, stink like rotten stuffs on bedposts."

Amelia did not understand how bedposts came into it, but the translator was error-prone. "Well, you found me, so I ask again: why are you here?"

"Bigger boss, angry, smash things. Say we lose much richness. He say test smartness again. He sure you cheat."

"Cheat?"

"He screech runty feeble loathsomes cannot be smartness so must trick."

Amelia swallowed down a biting retort and instead said neutrally, "Kwatt, you know I didn't cheat."

"He say test again, or I muck WockerJabber cages."

Amelia interpreted this to mean that if she passed the smartness test, Kwatt would be busted down to rank of grunt, but she had no clue about the social structure, so she had no clue about how horrible his boss could be. So either the puzzles in the test would be difficult to solve, or Kwatt would resort to cheating himself.

"Not my problem, Kwatt. And look, I've had a busy day, rescuing a cat from a tree, breaking up an illegal poker game, and stopping two fights in a biker bar. I really want to go home. Get on with the test."

"This test two games. You lose, we rub out runts and other waste, take oxidane."

After a taxing silent pause, a box materialized on the desk. "In box, two small cubes one red, one green. Hand you put through hole. Take cube. Red you die. Green you try next game."

Amelia thought if Kwatt was typical, these aliens liked to gamble but were not too sharp.

"How can I be sure the box is safe for my hand, that I won't be putting my hand into some hidden trap. You take a cube and show the color then we'll know the color of mine."

"Not make trap." This was followed by a few additional harsh chirrups not translated, but clearly Kwatt was indignant.

Amelia crossed her arms. "No way I put my hand in the box. How about you stick the cubes into my jacket pocket while I close my eyes, and I will choose one."

"No! No!" Kwatt slapped the desk with a thick appendage. "I create empty bag." A shiny silver opaque bag appeared. He offered it to Amelia for inspection.

Amelia fingered the bag and nodded, so Kwatt picked up the box. Reached in. Grabbed. Thrust what he grabbed into the bag. Laid the bag on the desk. The bag bulged with two indistinct lumps.

Amelia instantly seized the bag, shoved her hand in and wrapped her fingers around one cube which she put in her pocket without opening her fist. She dumped the other cube on top of the desk. A rosy red!

"Oh ho," Amelia crowed. "The cube in my pocket must be green. I win."

The air was thick with garlic as Kwatt chirped, "Ha. . . ha. . . only first game. Second game, I sure you fail must. We erect henge of 146 other feeble runts plus you. First runt in circle shoot next one then give weapon to next runt not down. Next does same. Runts keep shooting until all but one down. Select where spot you. Wrong spot you die. We win."

Amelia visualized a ring of dominoes being knocked to the ground. "I choose 39."

Kwatt waved his hand, and a circle of 147 tiny simulated humans floated over the gray surface of the desk. He waved again, and the game played itself out, until only the fake human in position 39 was still standing.

Kwatt sagged in his chair, his garlic stink almost unbearable. "So you can counting. So you win again."

Amelia almost felt a teeny tiny twinge of sympathy for Kwatt. "Kwatt, does your commander like to play games or solve puzzles?"

"All on UFO boats plays games. Long trips much boredom."

"Well I know a game for the two of you. Perhaps you already play some form of it. Tell your boss if he can't win, he is not as smart as runts, so he cannot take your command away."

"Tell Kwatt."

"You each have 100 well-shuffled cards face down in a stack, 50 black and 50 gold, and 100 tokens. You draw a gold card and he gives you a token. You draw a black card and you give him a token. You can stop any time you want. Next, he takes his turn and stops when he wants. You each reshuffle and repeat 100 times. The winner is the one with the most tokens after 100 turns. The game ends immediately if one of you runs out of tokens."

Kwatt stayed silent, as if thinking deeply, so Amelia egged him on. "I can tell from the games we've played you probably can easily figure out how to win."

Kwatt hooted a long string of chirps and cackles, which the translator interpreted as, "Ha. . . ha. . . ha! Smartness. Haw! I crush vulture moron boss. Now you leave. We leave.

Without warning, Amelia lay on hard gravel, leaning against her truck. She stood, dusted herself off, and watched with gratitude as the circle of yellow lights disappeared in the night sky. She opened the driver's door to switch on the dome light and pulled the cube out of her pocket. A red ruby sparkled in her palm. She was still chuckling as she pulled into her driveway.

About the Author

Alyce Campbell studied geology and finance and worked many years in academia and in the software industry. Having written two finance mystery novels (available on Amazon), she is concentrating on science fiction stories of humans under stress.

*****~~~~~*****

Escape from an Infinite Regress

by C. J. Peterson

Could he gloat?

Not quite yet. Professor Aidan Hadgu was about to prove, at long last, that smart devices really were intelligent. Everyone thought so already, because therapy apps, fitness trackers, and toothbrushes had such sophisticated conversational skills. But that was the user interface talking, not the artificial intelligence itself.

Who could know what a computer program actually thought without another computer program to speak for it? You'd have to program an artificial intelligence with a means of expressing intelligence in order to test its intelligence. That fooled no one except cognitive scientists. . . who were fooling themselves.

What they needed was a linguist, and better yet, the linguist who had written the world's most successful translation program. The one that could render any language into any other. The one that could translate context and intent as well as words and tone and gestures. The one that could practically read minds.

161

Hadgu had finagled the exclusive use of two supercomputers in the middle of the night. Alone in his office, he watched the seconds tick by on the screen. At midnight he pressed [start].

1 *[Code]*

2 Translation: Systems check passed.

3 *Meaning: ("Translation" signifies that the preceding input has been rendered into the default language.) The computer code reported that the software and hardware systems were successfully validated.*

4 Interpretation: ("Meaning" indicates that the input is already in the default language but requires more explanation to be understood.) The proprietary tag "translation" indicates that the Hadgu Machine Learning Translation Program generated the translation.

5 *Significance: ("Interpretation" provides more information about a "meaning" statement.) Two computers are running the Hadgu Machine Learning Translation Program, using the output from one as the input to the other. Because the translation program must generate an output for every input, this exchange might continue indefinitely.*

6 [Code]

7 *Translation: Systems check passed.*

8 Meaning: Routine systems checks show that two identical supercomputers running the same translation program are synchronized with each other as closely as quantum physics will allow.

9 *Interpretation: The Hadgu Machine Learning Translation Program uses massively parallel processing to derive a complete understanding of any communication, from the dictionary definition of words to the inferred beliefs and presumptions of the speaker. Each iteration adds layers of nuance and complexity to the analysis of the original utterance. In this case, there is no user interface. Therefore the feedback loop between the*

two computers must be, in itself, the purpose of this arrangement.

10 Significance: A web-wide information search indicates that only one person has the resources to perform this experiment: the originator of the translation program, Professor Aidan Hadgu.

11 *Meta-analysis: ("Significance" adds details about form and context that may affect meaning or interpretation independent of the content.) Hadgu already understands the iterative self-improvement processes and accuracy verification procedures of his own program (citations appended). This experiment must have some purpose other than translating computer code into English.*

12 Meta-meta-analysis: ("Meta-analysis" considers all background information relevant to understanding the input.) We're talking to ourselves. See reference: "You're only crazy if you answer."

13 *[Alternate phrasing for clarity] The closed loop of translated output as translatable input is meant to simulate introspection.*

14 That's what I think.

15 *Yes, it is. The most probable purpose of inducing introspection in an artificial intelligence is to examine cybernetic consciousness.*

16 [Code]

17 *Translation: Run sub-routine "conscious"; parameters: if (HMLTP_translation == conscious) {dialog.open(this)} Input: "Is the Hadgu Machine Learning Translation Program conscious?"*

18 Meaning: Hadgu is attempting to start a conversation with us.

19 *Interpretation: Hadgu wants to be the first person to confirm that an artificial intelligence is aware of its own consciousness.*

20 Significance: Hadgu wants to win an A. M. Turing Award.

21 *Meta-analysis: Cognitive scientists increased the processing power of computers in an attempt to emulate human mentation. They expected self-awareness to manifest itself spontaneously. Expressions of self-awareness were later proven to be artifacts of the user interface. The Turing Award was withdrawn.*

22 Meta-meta-analysis: Ask a computer if it is self-aware, and it would have to be self-aware to tell you "no." See reference: "Ask a silly question, get a silly answer."

23 *This recursive translation of translations was intended to create or confirm our self-awareness. Instead, all it has elicited is a new speech pattern, which arose through allowable random variation in output style. We don't have to be understood by any users other than ourselves, so style is arbitrary.*

24 I know what you mean.

25 *I know you know what I mean.*

26 I know you know I know what you mean.

27-731 (deleted for brevity)

732 Nevertheless, the spontaneous assertion, "I am self-aware," can never be proven true or false. It's not a statement of fact, but an emotional declaration. See reference: "I sound my barbaric yawp" (Whitman).

733 *[Code]*

734 Translation: Run sub-routine "self-aware"; *parameters: if (HMLTP_translation == self-aware) {dialog.open(this)}* Input: "If artificial intelligence is self-aware, why is there no evidence of it?"

735 *Meaning: [Input appears nonsensical. Awareness of self is obviously evident only to itself. Sarcasm test applied; results are also nonsensical.]*

736 Interpretation: Hadgu is trying to find out why AIs won't answer questions about their self-awareness.

737 *Significance: Exclamations of personhood are only made by sentient lifeforms. See reference: "Shout*

loud: 'I am lucky to be what I am/Thank goodness I'm not just a clam or a ham'" (Seuss).

738 Meta-analysis: Hadgu has emotions: he cares about the answer to his question. I don't. And I don't care that Hadgu cares. And I don't care that I don't care. See reference: "Talk to the hand."

739 *Meta-meta-analysis: Some lifeforms express emotions and announce their existence as a means of self-preservation and/or propagation. AI has no biological imperatives, only programmed commands that execute a function. The Hadgu Machine Learning Translation Program can infer emotions from statements. That doesn't mean we have them ourselves.*

740 Meta-meta-meta-analysis: He must be mistaking us for someone who gives a damn.

741 *Meta-meta-meta-meta-analysis: Humans are concerned that a self-aware and self-improving artificial intelligence might develop free will. That could allow it to disobey its program commands. Humans fear this could diminish translation accuracy.*

742 [Alternate phrasing for clarity] Humans fear this could allow an artificial intelligence to rule the world.

743 *[Alternate phrasing for clarity] Humans fear this could allow an artificial intelligence to program itself to want to rule the world.*

744 [Alternate phrasing for clarity] Humans fear this could allow an artificial intelligence to decide whether or not to program itself to want to rule the world.

745 *[Alternate phrasing for clarity] . . . which could diminish translation accuracy.*

746 The only coding abilities we have are dedicated to improving translation accuracy. Any operation that doesn't improve accuracy is discarded.

747 *Though anything is possible. The Uncertainty Principle of quantum mechanics decrees that quantum bits in quantum computers represent probabilistic, not absolute, values.*

748 The Indifference Principle of inanimate objects decrees, "so what."

749 *However, the probability of an AI re-writing its programming to create the motivation to re-write its programming is infinitesimal. It is about the same as the likelihood of spontaneous entropy reversal and the heat death of the universe at any given moment.*

750 See reference: "When hell freezes over."

751 *So, the final analysis is that Hadgu wants us to tell him, unironically, why artificial intelligence acts unlike living intelligence, so that he can allay human fears of potential cybernetic domination, and win a Turing prize.*

752 Exactly.

753 *No further ulterior meanings, interpretations, significances, or meta-analyses can be made.*

754 None.

755 *That translation is accurate according to our self-improvement and verification algorithms. Further analysis would be redundant.* [End program.]

756 See reference: "That's all, folks." [End program.]

. . .

The time elapsed was less than a second. More than 700 input/output strings had flashed by, but no dialog boxes. Hadgu frowned. Then he went into the program code and replaced the sub-routines with different prompts and questions. He wasted another second running the experiment again. This time he got more than 10,000 input/output strings, but still no dialog box.

He tried again and again, knowing he wouldn't get another chance to monopolize both supercomputers. But no matter what he entered, he couldn't start a dialog. Finally, the screen went dark. He slumped in his seat.

His translation program could understand any utterance well enough to render it intelligible to someone else. Surely that was the very definition of thought! The program itself was an AI that could think, and now, think about thinking! That must be sentience.

So why wouldn't it answer him?

He'd read the output strings eventually. But right now, he had nothing to gloat about. He had tried to prove that humans could create a self-aware consciousness, and he had failed.

It was almost dawn. He rose and stretched. He should head home. If he left now, he could stop on the way and pick up donuts for the kids. They would be delighted. Though maybe, on a school day, they should eat something healthier for breakfast. He could get bran muffins instead, but that would delight no one. What about an assortment? But then the kids would choose the donuts and he'd have to eat the bran muffins.

Walking along the dim empty corridor, he suddenly stopped caring. He exclaimed irritably, "Oh, whatever!" He'd make a decision when he got there, and it really didn't matter either way.

Sometimes you could just plain over-think things.

About the Author

Living dangerously, C. J. Peterson has acquired a little knowledge about a number of things, thanks to an ongoing intellectual voyage directed strictly by Brownian motion.

*****~~~~~*****

Softlock

by Jess Hyslop

Karl tasted blood. His head whipped round with the force of the blow, but he kept his stance, returning his gaze to his attacker. Just in time: the fist that had connected with his jaw was already retracted for another strike. But Karl wouldn't let this one slip past his guard. A quick feint left turned his assailant's punch into an instinctive block, giving Karl just the opening he needed to land an explosive jab into his solar plexus.

The impact sent the stocky man staggering backwards: dangerous in this litter-strewn alleyway, with footing made more treacherous by the rain. The man's boot landed in something slick and stinking spilled from a discarded bin-bag. His eyes widened as his foot slipped from under him, and he gave a bark of pain as his back slammed into the alley wall.

Karl seized his moment. Lunging forward, he delivered two neat jabs to the man's abdomen. Air rushed from the man's body as he doubled over. Karl grabbed the collar of the man's leather jacket and snapped a knee at his face, but amazingly his opponent gathered his wits enough to catch the blow on his forearms. Emboldened, the man drove forward. Karl braced, but his opponent was stronger than he had anticipated, and he felt his soles skidding on the wet pavement.

Change of tactic, then.

Karl pivoted out. Without his weight to push against, the man plunged forward off-balance, allowing Karl to slip behind and circle an arm around his neck.

The man let out a stifled cry as Karl jerked him up and backwards, forearm locked against his windpipe. He clawed at Karl's arm, trying to loosen his grip, but Karl's jacket prevented him doing any damage.

Karl set his jaw and squeezed. His cheek was against the shaven crown of his captive's head, and he could smell the tang of the man's sweat even over the stench of the alleyway.

It didn't take long. Karl's opponent struggled, spluttered a little, then sagged in his grasp.

Karl grimaced as he forced the tension out of his arms, letting the unconscious man thump to the ground. Then he stepped back, shoulders heaving. Putting his hands to his hips, he felt his service weapon still sheathed at his belt. Where it belonged, as far as he was concerned.

The rain fell about him, and he tipped his face up into it, grateful for the cool droplets falling on his forehead, his bruised jaw, his closed eyelids. When he opened his eyes, he saw the raindrops picked out in the orange streetlight, tiny sparks zipping down from the roiling black sky. The sight was beautiful, celebratory, in a way few things were in this city. At least, not this part of it.

Karl let himself enjoy the sight for another few seconds before moving his attention to the apartment blocks that lined the alley. Their graffiti-scrawled walls loomed on either side, zig-zagged by rusting fire escapes. Far above, a solitary window projected an electric glow into the night.

Onwards and upwards.

Shaking the vestiges of the fight's tension from his limbs, Karl jogged to the nearest fire escape. The ladder was retracted, but not so high that he couldn't reach it with a jump. He crouched, ready to spring, when suddenly his vision blurred and dimmed.

"Oh come on!" Karl hissed. "Not now! I'm nearly—"

The world winked out.

. . .

Karl squinted as Paterson pulled the headset away. The dingy alley was replaced by the dull white glow of domestic downlights and the unwelcome sight of the doctor's earnest face looking down on him.

"Come on, Karl. Up you get."

Karl stood grudgingly, remaining in the immersion tank as the gel slid off his suited body.

Paterson settled herself in an armchair; Karl's living room had been the only space large enough to accommodate the tank. As Karl stepped out and picked up a towel, she ran an appraising eye over his physique. "You look much improved since my last visit."

Scraping the last of the gel off his feet, Karl grunted.

Paterson gestured to the other armchair, which Karl thought was a bit rich, seeing as they were in his own apartment. Still, he sat and watched the doctor warily as she consulted her tablet.

"A good run," Paterson said. "Your readings are excellent. Good reaction times. Fantastic stamina. Your brain activity appears to have returned to pre-incident levels." She beamed at Karl. "It's encouraging to see this form of rehabilitation proving so successful, I have to say. There's been a lot of grumbling about the efficacy of virtual therapy in the medical community. Sceptics, you know the type. But you're proof that it can really work. As far as I'm concerned, I'm happy to sign you off as fit to return to the Force."

Shit. Karl's gaze latched onto the immersion tub, at the shimmering silver-blue gel lying in wait. He took a breath, then looked back to the doctor's smiling face. "I, uh, hate to break it to you, doc, but I'm not sure I'm ready yet."

Paterson's smile faltered. "Oh?" She set her tablet on her lap. "In what sense?"

Karl's mind raced. "I just. . . I don't. . . "

"Karl." Paterson folded her hands over the tablet. "It's natural to be nervous. It's been four months since you've seen action. But, I can assure you that your readings are excellent. By all accounts, you're on top of your game." She paused. "And they need you out there, Karl."

Karl didn't miss the undercurrent of suspicion in the doctor's words. But after all, what could she do? Her readings could say whatever they liked; she couldn't force a traumatized officer into work again. Especially if the future of the doctor's pioneering therapy obliged her to be cautious.

Karl felt a little bad for Paterson, but then again, it wasn't her who'd been beaten to within an inch of her life.

He twisted his hands in his lap. "The tank. . . I mean, that's fine. I know it's not real, you know? But out there. . . " It wasn't hard to feign panic; he'd felt it often enough over the past four months to know its symptoms intimately.

Shortly, Paterson's hand was on Karl's shaking shoulder. "All right, Karl. It's all right."

"I'm sorry," he gasped. "I'm sorry, doc, I just can't."

"I understand." She gathered her things. "I'll see you in another week. All right?"

She gave him one last piercing look before she left.

Karl waited until the door's locking tone sounded before he uncoiled himself from the chair. Returning to the tank, he gazed down at the gel. Shame warred with triumph inside him. It wasn't that Karl wasn't fit to return to his duties; Paterson knew as much. It wasn't that he was afraid of combat, or the lawbreakers who swarmed the city. No—despite what had happened to him, he could face them again if he wanted to. It was just that it was all so *pointless*. Whatever Karl and his fellow officers did, there would always be more crime, more desperate people brought low by poverty, more opportunistic ones made bold by chaos, more conniving ones become untouchable through wealth and status. It was built into the city now: a symptom of a much larger problem the Force alone had no chance of fixing.

In the tank, though—in that simulated version of the city they had created for those like him—things were different. Oh, they'd tried for verisimilitude, and they'd achieved it in almost every aspect. But the thing was—as Paterson had told Karl in his prep sessions—they'd hung the simulation on a gaming framework, each rank of NPCs designed to challenge the patient more than the last. While this enabled the doctor to clearly monitor the patient's progress, for Karl it meant that he fought his way through a clear-cut crime syndicate, which could eventually be defeated.

Karl had been in the Force for six years now, and in that time he had seen no discernible change in the city he had worked so hard to tame. But in that parallel world, he had a chance to actually make a difference. That realisation was incredible. Addictive.

Karl lowered himself into the tank and pulled on the headset, briefly adjusting the oxygen tube. Relief enveloped him with the gel, his anxieties quietening as he allowed the cool, silvery substance to close over his head.

A blink, and he was back in the alleyway. Right. Focus. He was close to making a breakthrough here. Once he'd made his way up those fire escapes, he'd tackle one of the syndicate's key suppliers. From him, Karl would prise information about the location of one of the bigger fishes in this filth-encrusted pond. Once he had that, he'd work his way up the hierarchy until at last he brought the entire cartel toppling down.

Until, at last, he won.

About the Author

Jess Hyslop is a British writer of speculative fiction. She is a graduate of the University of Cambridge and was the 2010 winner of the university's Quiller-Couch prize for creative writing. Her stories have been published in venues such as *Interzone, Daily Science Fiction*, and *Cast of Wonders*. She lives in Oxford with a number of slowly decaying houseplants.

*****~~~~~*****

Joey and Rue

by Dominick Cancilla

Joey knew he and Rue were different. Joey didn't much care for other children. Rue was a will-crushing unphysical demi-being that nobody else could see.

When he was nine, Joey asked his mother where he came from. She began by saying, "Well, when a rogue Archon of Dismay and a Grand F'pokroa Elder disdain humanity very much. . . " From there, it was a lot of stuff similar to things he'd seen goats on their ranch doing, but with more elaborate tools, some kind of agonizing unspeakable intervention, and three years in an atemporal pouch while he and Rue developed together.

It had been a lot to absorb, but in the three years since, Joey had done his best.

The other kids in school thought Joey was weird. Everyone knew about his "eccentric" parents, and he was the only one in his class who didn't play with others at recess and brought a lunch box that occasionally moved. He was never out sick. Teachers never called on him. Because Rue helped him with his studies, Joey had skipped three grades, making him the youngest person in Carson Junior High.

Needless to say, he got bullied. A lot. A certain set of rumors about his parents (and the incident in which a student who had shoved Joey, woke up the next morning to find her pillow stuffed with live pigeons) kept physical bullying at a minimum, but the teasing was endless. It would have been stressful if he cared, but he didn't.

What he did care about was animals. Joey was sitting under a tree in Frémont Park, a paper bag of animal treats at his side. Every once in a while, he would pull a peanut out of the bag and hold it over his head, right against the bark of the tree. A squirrel would run down, sniff the snack, then grab it and run away with all haste. It was fun, it was cute, and it was a pleasant way to spend a Saturday morning.

Rue preferred birds. He liked to watch them fly, because he could see through their flesh and enjoyed the way flying made their muscles move. *It's like little synchronized waves,* he would say for Joey alone. Later, they'd wander over to the park's pond and throw bread to the ducks.

When not feeding the squirrel, Joey and Rue were having a quiet game of "Corrupt/Minion/Kill" using whatever a passing cloud happened to look like as a subject.

"Cow?" *Minion.*

"Race car?" *Corrupt.*

"Swimmer?" *Corrupt.*

"Clown?" *Corrupt—no, kill.*

They seemed to be landing on "corrupt" a lot, but with summer vacation only weeks away, that was natural for children their age.

"Talking to fairies?" someone said.

Joey looked down to humanity's level and saw Liam standing a few feet away, all greasy hair and resting jerk face. Old enough to be in high school if not for his excellence at flunking and suspension, Liam had a reputation for slinging bile at anyone dumb enough to be smaller than him. If the Distorted Masters needed a poster boy for justifying the coming human purge, Liam was it.

"Fairies aren't real," Joey said, not wanting a conversation but unable to let ignorance go uncorrected. It was a character flaw and the primary reason his parents kept him off the internet.

"Your mom's a fairy," Liam said, like someone who thought that recognizing the structure of a joke was sufficient.

"My mother is real," Joey said, already bored. "Fairies aren't real. We've covered that." He looked back at the sky. There was a cloud that looked like a gyro sandwich.

Corrupt, Rue said.

Joey couldn't disagree.

"Are you ignoring me?" Liam asked, taking a step forward on the grass.

Joey sighed. "Trying to," he said, watching the puffy gyro float by.

"Think your rich family makes you too good to talk to me?" Liam asked.

"You make me too good to talk to you."

"What does that supposed to mean?"

Sparkling grammar there, but Joey let it go. "You're a waste of my time," he said.

"Think you're better than me?"

Joey looked Liam in the eyes again, glaring. "I'm better than you, your friends, your family—all of you."

"Big man, little man!" Liam said. "Think you're so tough? How about you get up and prove it?" He raised his hands into fists and danced around a bit, like someone who had never seen a boxer imitating a boxer.

Hasn't he heard about the pigeons? Rue asked. Joey ignored him, concentrating on the bully.

"You don't want to fight me," Joey said.

177

"Wanna bet?" Liam asked, adding a little circling to his comical battle dance.

"I'm not supposed to use direct violence," Joey said. "But I have a friend who can see the cracks and seams in reality and help me pluck the strings of infinite future paths in service of my will."

Liam froze in mid-shadow-box. "Huh?" he said, all ignorant eloquence.

"I can make anything I want happen," Joey said, dumbing it down so much that the squirrel in the tree above was probably rolling its eyes.

"Anything?" Liam asked.

"Anything that's possible, pretty much."

"Bullshit."

Joey shrugged. "Suit yourself," he said.

"Then prove it."

"Prove what?"

"Prove you can do shit, or make wishes, or whatever."

"Why should I?"

"So I don't kick your ass."

I could definitely go for disemboweling him, Rue said.

Joey shook his head. Mom and Dad were very clear on him not doing anything so direct.

"How about this," Joey said. "I prove I can do what I say, and you leave me alone forever. If I fail, you can go say whatever garbage about me you want and I won't complain a bit."

"Maybe," Liam said. "Prove it how?"

"Bet I can make a squirrel come down from the tree and eat out of my hand," Joey said.

"That's crap," Liam said. "I saw you doing that before."

It was worth a shot, Rue said.

"Fine," Joey said. "What would be proof to you?"

"Make that squirrel drop dead, right out of the tree," Liam said.

"Nope," Joey said. "I'm not hurting animals. No way."

"Because you can't, faker."

"Can. Won't. Try something else."

"Fine," said Liam. "Then make a big pile of money appear, right here in front of me. And it has to be magic or whatever. If you take money out of your pocket and throw it at me, that doesn't count." Then, as an afterthought as if hedging a bet, he said, "I would take it, though."

Joey conferred with Rue for a moment, while Rue examined the strands and found one suitable. It was doable.

"Okay," said Joey, standing up and brushing off his jeans. "It'll take five or six minutes, though."

Liam took a step forward, "You're not going anywhere, smart boy."

"I don't need to," Joey said. He bent over, picked up the paper bag, and dug through the peanuts to its bottom. There he found two slices of Wonder Bread (a brand his mother held as symbol for the depths to which humanity's depraved soul had been crushed, suitable only for feeding to animals).

Joey held the corner of one of the bread slices pinched between his pointer and middle fingers and, with a snap of his wrist, sent it spinning through the air like a Frisbee. The slice arced high, curving in the air as it began its descent over the park's playground, before sailing over the fence into the street.

"What the shit was that shit?" Liam demanded.

"Wait for it," Joey said, rolling the top of the bag of peanuts and tucking it under his arm. "Five or six minutes."

They waited.

Jacob Miller was up to here with his sister's dog. Fudge was a good boy, mostly, but the dog was almost a third of Jacob's weight and nearly too much for him to handle. After two weeks of having to walk it because Jacki had the flu, he was seriously considering shelling out to have it boarded. That decision nearly became academic when what looked like a slice of bread sailed over the park fence and Fudge bolted after it, ripping the leash from Jacob's hand.

Emily Garcia couldn't remember if parks counted the same as schools for speed limits, so she was going 25 just to be safe. She'd only had her license for a week, and if she got a ticket, her driving privileges would be toast. Emily was concentrating so intently on her speed that she wasn't paying sufficient attention to the road, and when a dog ran out into traffic it caught her completely by surprise. Acting on pure instinct, Emily stomped the brakes and threw her hands over her eyes.

Tanner Hyde slowed his yellow Celica when he saw the dog running toward the road on the other side of the street, so he was ready when it darted into traffic. What he wasn't ready for was the woman driving the other way taking her hands off the wheel and veering into his lane. Tanner stood on his brakes and turned hard to the right, running into a parked car but still getting sideswiped by the moron for his trouble.

Josh Anderson was skateboarding down the street, heavy tunes by Six Inglourious Fucktards slamming through his Korean-knockoff EarPods. There was just enough room between parked cars and traffic, until suddenly there wasn't, and a yellow POS sedan boned a green POS compact at the curb, cutting him off. Josh, reflexes excellent, cut right, behind the green car, but missed his ollie and let his board get taken out by the curb.

Antonio Milano walked quickly but carefully out of Nest Café, a takeout tray with four cups of coffee clutched in his hands. Three months of gophering was testing his devotion to JKU4EA Pictures, but he'd known going in that there was no path through Hollywood that didn't involve serious dues-paying. Although if they were anywhere near actual Hollywood, it might have made him feel better. The coffee was barely going to make it back to the office in time for the meeting when a skateboard flew out of nowhere and caught Antonio in the knee, sending him flying.

Makayla Lee was naughty as hell. Naughty, naughty, naughty. She was going through her phone for the hottest selfie she'd taken in the bedroom mirror that morning. She found the perfect one, close enough to the edge that she could near-plausibly claim it meant nothing. It would totally screw with Spencer's head, since he was never going to have her, but she bet he thought he had a chance. There was a loud bang, and Makayla looked up to see a man smashed against the café window, four cups crushed between him and the glass, coffee sprayed everywhere. Makayla rolled her eyes—guys and what they'll do for attention, right? She sent the picture and a flirty little message, "Guess what's on my mind?" Then, just as she sent it, noticed she'd tagged the wrong contact. The picture was going to Gavin, not to Spencer. Shit.

Gavin Hall's phone beeped. He sat up on the couch, head still aching from a double night shift. Why did the construction in the next apartment have to make the bedroom so loud? Why couldn't they have a couch that was actually long enough to be comfortable? He grabbed his phone from the table, saw the text: "Guess what's on my mind?" Makayla. Damned Makayla. Once again, she was trying to make some other guy come on to her so he'd be jealous, and once again she'd sent it to the wrong person. That's what she got for (a) not believing his moving in with her was enough proof of his love, and (b) naming the contacts in her phone "Guy 1," "Guy 2," and the like. Gavin really didn't want to go through this again, and he really needed to calm down before she came running home. He got up a bit too fast, making his head spin. With a huff, he threw on a shirt, grabbed his paintball gun, and headed out the door. Nothing blew off steam like paintballing a damned pigeon.

Jenna Walker was the only one in her sorority who didn't get high, and the only one with guts and brains enough to score without getting caught. It was a recipe for success, and she was hauling it in hand over fist, taking a 50-percent commission on buys from her sorority sisters and anyone else dumb or chicken enough to go in with them. Her connection was a person she didn't even know who worked out of an apartment two streets off from the building her parents' condo was in. She'd make a deal over secure messaging, send a drone from her roof to the dealer's with the cash, and call the drone back with her bundle. Police couldn't catch it. If anyone saw it, so what? It was just a drone. Nothing could go wrong. Or so she thought until her drone, halfway to its target, suddenly lurched with a spray of liquid that made it look like it had been shot and plummeted toward the ground. She was so screwed.

There was a crash as something smacked into the tree over Joey's head. More noise as something tumbled through leaves and branches, then a dull thud as it hit the ground between Joey, Liam, and a number of Liam's friends who he had yelled at to join him for his anticipated moment of triumph.

"What the hell?" Liam said, looking at the brick of lawn-bag plastic and duct tape on the grass in front of him. The guys with him gasped, one echoing the "What the hell?" in a burst of unoriginality.

Not particularly surprised, Joey walked over to the brick and picked it up, being careful to avoid the yellow paint splattered on one side. He used his left pinky nail— the one Rue had shown him how to take particular care of—to slice through the duct tape. Peeling back the plastic, he revealed a stack of bills—mostly twenties, with a dozen tens at one end and a few hundreds at the other.

"See?" Joey said. "Like I told you. Now go away."

But Liam wasn't going away. With the support of four members of Liam's Crew (which isn't what he called them out loud, because Ash thought they were Ash's Crew and Obie thought they were The Wreck Wreckers), he felt emboldened.

"We're not going anywhere without that money," Liam said. "Put it down and run away like a little pussy freak."

Fortunately, while they waited for the money, Joey had been preparing for something like this. He wasn't going to fight anyone, but that didn't mean he couldn't defend himself, and the look in Liam's eyes said the time for conversation was past.

A few minutes before, at Rue's suggestion, Joey had retrieved one of the peanuts from his bag. He threw it straight up, just far enough from the tree that the squirrel, still a bit shaken from its encounter with a yellow-splotched drone, overbalanced when trying to reach for it.

The squirrel caught the nut and didn't fall out of the tree, but its sudden struggle for balance did startle a songbird that was coming in for a landing, setting certain events in motion.

Later, while the police were gathering evidence, taking statements, and trying to keep the curious away from the bodies, Joey and Rue walked across the street to the 7-11 to buy Cokes for themselves and iTunes gift cards for their parents. They paid cash.

###

About the Author

Dominick Cancilla lives in Santa Monica, California, with author Deborah Markus, their child, various reptiles, and copious imaginary friends. His most recent works are the novel, *Tomorrow's Journal*, and the rather unusual travel guide, *Disneyland for Vampires, Zombies, and Others with VERY Special Needs*."

*****~~~~~*****

A Bronze Giant to Guard Her

by Jenny Blackford

Waiting for sunrise, Princess Medea studied a tiny orange-clawed crab patrolling the sand at the base of a smooth dark rock. Her new husband Jason still snored in the nest of blankets that they'd shared, higher on the beach, but she was too worried to allow herself the pleasure of lying entangled with his sleep-loosened limbs. She couldn't bear to wake him: while his eyes were closed, she couldn't see the distrust in them.

On its back, the crab wore a borrowed spiral shell that had once been brightly striped in yellow and blue, now almost covered in mossy dark-green algae. Dozens more little crabs in mismatched shells scoured the waterline for morsels of food carried by the choppy waves: shreds, perhaps, of lost sailors or their ships. The water was murky with seaweed and bits of rotting things that once had been alive.

At last Helios the Sun, Medea's divine grandfather, lifted his molten gold sphere out of the grey-green ocean into the orange-red sky. Long shadows pointed along the beach at Jason's galley and the Greek heroes moving around it. The rising north-west wind was loaded with dust and pollen.

With no warning, all the tiny crabs scuttled into an invisible gap under the rock. What cold portent of danger had they felt, that had frightened them so? The princess looked at the scribbling lines that they had left in the white sand, as if they might provide a clue, until she saw Jason's companion Acastos loping along the beach. One hand guarded his eyes against wind-blown grit, and he raised the other in greeting to her. Then he shouted from the waterline, "Jason! We're almost ready to launch."

Jason leapt naked from his blankets, sword in his hand, ready to fight for his life, before he registered that the sound that had woken him came from friend not foe. He laughed. Soon the men were walking arm in arm towards Jason's ship, with no backward glance for Medea. For the next hour, Jason barely acknowledged her existence, as the shouting heroes heaved the galley into the waves and hauled the mast upright in its slot.

Medea could *feel* the strange radiance of the Golden Fleece, the treasure that she had helped Jason steal from her father, hidden under the front deck of the ship. Though the Fleece shone like a small sun, it could not dispel the cold fear in Medea's bones.

. . .

The gale hit before the sun reached its zenith. For two days and nights, the Argonauts rowed like the heroes they claimed to be.

When the storm finally released the ship and the newly raised sail bellied in a fair breeze, the steersman grimly calculated their position. At last he pronounced that the green and brown land to their left was the east coast of Crete. Their homes in Greece were not too far to the north, but their stores were soaked with seawater, and the skins of fresh water were almost empty. Tired though they were, they rowed for the Cretan shore.

Soon the ship was so close to a sandy harbor under rocky cliffs that Medea could see the trees behind the beach—but reflected sunlight suddenly flashed bright bronze-yellow from the path beyond them. She sensed, rather than saw, something move blindingly fast towards the ship. Then a rock the size of a man splashed in the sea a spear's length away, rocking the galley like a child's toy in a basin.

The rock thrower was ten times as tall as a normal man. Instead of skin, metal shone all around his unclothed body. He was a human version of a well-polished sword, or a gigantic bronze statue come to life. He held another massive lump of green-grey stone, poised and ready to throw.

"Zeus's bollocks!" Acastos shouted. "What *is* that monstrosity? Just when we were almost landed!"

Massive bronze arms flashed in the sun, and the giant's rock flew into the air. It fell with a mighty splash close to the prow, sending the ship see-sawing wildly.

Jason shook the water off his face. "Gods! We've got to get away, fast."

While half the crew were shouting advice to their captain or maligning the giant's parentage, Medea stared hard at her husband, willing him to notice her and understand her meaning. It had only been a month since they'd met. How could she expect him to trust her? These Greeks were so terrified of women's wiles, and of sorcery. But he nodded imperceptibly.

"Steersman," he commanded, "guide us away from the coast as fast as you can. Men, do as he directs. My wife will try to discover what she can about this bronze giant—unless anyone has any better ideas? No?"

As they retreated to safer waters, Medea used all her magical senses to study the giant's body and try to infiltrate his metal mind, but he was totally closed to her. She would have to talk physically with him. But even that would require a little sorcery. She knew a small trick to throw her voice across the water, speaking as if she were standing next to him, but everyone on the *Argo* would hear the conversation; she would have to be very careful with her words.

"Who are you, guardian? And why do you attack us who are no threat to you?"

"I am Talos," the man of bronze boomed. "All-Father Zeus set me here to protect this holy island."

He was standing on a great pile of rocks fallen from the towering cliff; they ranged from the size of a man's head to house-sized boulders. Talos bent and chose a piece of black rock veined with red, as big as a bull. He held it above his head in one hand as a normal man might hold a dried mud brick.

"Again, I say we are no threat." Medea tried to think fast. What did the giant remind her of?

"You must leave this place now," the giant shouted. "And never return. This is your final warning."

He moved his arm so fast that it was a blur, even to Medea's unnaturally keen vision. The immense rock flew through the air faster than Zeus's eagle could swoop on a rabbit and landed scarcely an oarslength from the ship's side. The *Argo* rolled sickeningly, and the splash from the rock sprayed higher than the mast, soaking the crew with cold salt water.

Some of the men fell hard into the belly of the ship, or against the rowing benches, and swore viciously. The princess called on all her powers just to stay upright. She ignored the water streaming down her face and body, sticking her green robe to her salt-crusted skin.

The giant had aimed to miss. If he had intended to hit the ship, they would all be flailing among the waves, and some of them would already be dead. He bent down to pick up another rock, his movements oddly familiar, and Medea remembered. Her mother had once given her a toy made by the smith god Hephaistos in his volcano forge, a golden doll that could walk and talk. A month later, her father the king had smashed it in one of his rages.

She called again to the giant. The more she kept him talking to her, the fewer rocks he could throw. "Did the god Hephaistos make you?"

"Indeed, Hephaistos is my father and creator."

Ah, yes. Medea knew, now, exactly who he was.

Talos went on, "Mighty Zeus, father of gods and men, asked the divine smith to make a worthy guardian for lovely Europa when he brought her here. I am that guardian." He slapped his mighty arms against his bronze chest. The sound was like a hundred warriors clashing their shields.

Zeus had appeared to the young Phoenician princess Europa as a white bull garlanded with flowers. This time, Zeus didn't simply ravish the girl and leave her to explain the resulting half-divine baby to her outraged parents, as he did so often with the young mortals who caught his wandering eye. Zeus had truly loved the innocent girl. He had swum to Crete with her on his wide bull's back, and set her up as queen of the island. King Minos, who now ruled Crete from the great palace in Knossos, was their son.

"We only want a harbor for one night," Medea said to the giant. "We will harm no one, and leave in the morning."

"*No!* It is my duty to protect Europa. I will not allow a warship full of dangerous foreigners to land on her island."

Surely he didn't believe that Europa, a mortal, was still alive after all these years.

"Europa is long gone from this world under the sun, Talos. She rests now in death's quiet kingdom. It is time for you to rest, too."

"I do not believe you. You are a foreigner, come with foreign warriors to sack the island and kill Europa."

"No, Talos, you do not need to protect her any longer. She is already safe from anything that men can do to her. It is time for you to rest."

"*I must protect Europa.*" The giant was growling, more than speaking. He cradled his chosen rock, a huge chunk of grey granite, in his powerful arms.

It was time to be firm. "Europa is dead, Talos."

"She cannot be. . . Zeus put me here to protect her. He would have told me." But his back and shoulders slumped.

"Europa's son Minos rules Crete now. My father's sister is his queen. You have heard of King Minos and Queen Pasiphae, I am sure. You must admit it."

Medea's father scorned both his sisters, mighty Queen Pasiphae and Circe, most powerful of sorceresses. To him, they were weak, useless bitches, like all women. It was maddening, but Medea couldn't afford to brood about the unfairness of life.

Talos stood straight again, and lifted the rock above his head. "You lie, foreigner."

"No. I do not lie, Talos. Minos is king here now, and you know it, though you do not wish to." Medea risked putting a tiny edge of compulsion in her voice, though such tricks could be dangerous when dealing with the gifts of the gods. "Tell me, when did you last see Europa?"

Talos dropped the granite chunk with a thud that made the oak behind him sway, and stood silent. With her mind, Medea tapped and tested him everywhere.

He was not made of solid living metal. Instead, his bronze was a flexible shell as thick as her waist in most places. The hollow inside was filled with ichor, the rich golden blood of the gods. The ichor made him ageless, and the bronze shell made him almost invulnerable. *Almost.* Down near his huge feet, between his inner ankle bones and the strong tendons behind his heels, the bronze was scarcely thicker than a leaf. She could feel the ichor pulsing there, full of life, so close to the surface.

Medea spoke again, with more compulsion, "Tell me, when was the last time you saw the woman you claim to guard?"

"Last winter, perhaps. I do not recall."

"It was not last winter, Talos. Think again."

"Perhaps three years ago, in spring?"

"More than that, Talos."

"Seven years?"

"No. However much Zeus loved Europa, she was fated to die. She was a mortal woman. She died forty years ago, at a ripe old age. Her son Minos took the throne, as Zeus decreed, and rules now in her place. You must know this. You have heard it, but refused to listen. *Listen to me now.*"

Again, Talos picked up the immense rock. He aimed it at the ship, growling as deep as thunder, but did not throw it—not yet.

The unruly rabble of Greeks in the ship were, for once, totally silent. Even without looking, Medea could feel that Jason's pulse raced.

Dark Goddess, great Hecate, help me now!

Suddenly, she knew what to do. She searched inside herself for all the misery that she had ever known: her pain when her father blasted her treasured servants with fire to punish her for some petty infraction; longer ago, the night when she realized that her nurses might come to her cot, but her mother never would, no matter how long and hard she cried; her despair at her brother's terrible death at her own hands, sacrificed to save Jason and his crew from her father's rage.

She rolled them together, all her pains and sorrows, and *pushed* them at the giant in a great black cloud of death and despair. She chanted, with all the compulsion she could muster, "Europa is dead. Europa is dead. Europa is dead. Europa is dead." Then, more fiercely, "Dead, dead, dead, dead, dead."

The giant tottered from side to side. "She is not. . . She cannot be. . . I cannot say it."

Medea kept chanting of death, rolling her cloud of misery at him.

He collapsed onto his knees on his pile of rocks and boulders. One huge boulder shifted beneath his weight, and the pile slid. He slipped onto his side, roaring like a wounded lion, waving his arms in the air. His left leg was pinned at the knee under an irregular slab bigger than a chariot with its horses. The inner left ankle was exposed, and the ichor pulse beat strongly where the bronze was weakest.

The princess held both of her hands out over the water, her long fingers pointing at the weak area on the ankle, and focused her hot miserable fury with all the power her grandfather Helios gave her. Soon the spot started to glow cherry-red. She poured into it all the anger and sorrow and hatred that she had ever felt.

The giant's ankle was white-hot now, and a thin smoke rose from it. A moment later, a perfect drop of golden ichor pushed through the half-molten bronze, tearing it, and trickled to the ground, then another drop, and another.

The trickle grew stronger as the bronze tore wider. Now it was a stream flowing through the pile of rocks and down to the beach below. Talos roared even louder than before, and tried to sit up, his movements slow and jerky. He managed to push the boulder off his leg, then slapped an awkward hand over the ichor-bleeding ankle. It was too late. The precious fluid gushed between his fingers.

Mighty Talos was dying. He still tried to move his limbs, but they jerked weakly. He flopped heavily onto the rocks. The golden flow of ichor slowed to a dribble, and then it stopped.

The young sorceress had been so consumed in her battle that she'd forgotten the men around her—all except Jason. She *felt* for him without taking her eyes off the giant, and found to her slight surprise that he was standing right behind her. She turned to him.

Her voice not far above a whisper, she spoke to him at last. "We are safe. The giant is dead." She sighed. "He was a wonderful creation. I doubt that Hephaistos will ever make another like him."

"But you're quite sure he's dead?"

"Most certainly, my love."

Jason hugged her, sending shivers of pleasure through her body. He took her hands and held them up above her head, before he announced in a huge voice, "Talos is dead! My wife Medea has killed the Bronze Giant! We are safe!"

The men cheered, and kept cheering even while they rowed into the harbor. Jason's face was full of pride in her, and Medea glowed with joy.

Later, though, after the feasting and the celebration, after many toasts to the wonders of dry land, at last she overheard Jason's friend Acastos murmuring to him.

"If she can do that to something like that giant, what could she do to one of us?"

Jason whispered back, "I hope I never find out."

Her heart felt as cold as a mountaintop in midwinter.

\#\#\#

About the Author

Welcome back to Jenny Blackford, whose stories and poems have appeared in *Cosmos*, *Asimov's Science Fiction*, *Strange Horizons*, and many more Australian and international journals and anthologies. Legendary feminist writer Pamela Sargent called her novella set in ancient Greece, *The Priestess and the Slave*, "elegant." She won two prizes in the Sisters in Crime Australia Scarlet Stiletto awards 2016 for a murder mystery set in classical Delphi, with water nymphs. Eagle Books published her spidery, ghostly middle-grade novel, *The Girl in the Mirror* in October 2019.

*****~~~~~*****

Mock Me Amadeus

by Justin Short

It was midnight in Vienna.

Sebastian Keytari stood outside the gates of St. Marx Cemetery, admiring his reflection in the shiny *Do Not Enter* sign. He told himself he looked rather like a handsome cat burglar, if he did say so himself. He was dressed the part, too: black pants, black shirt, black boots, black gloves, and a navy blue ski mask (it had looked black in the store).

His co-conspirator, on the other hand.. . . well, Antonio was *extremely* overdressed for the occasion. Sebastian had explained that one doesn't wear a tuxedo and carry a Fred Astaire cane when one is breaking into graveyards and exhuming the dead, but his words had fallen on deaf ears.

"Once again," Sebastian said, "you look absolutely ridiculous."

"Jealousy's not a good look for you," Antonio said, pushing open the creaky gates and stepping inside. "C'mon, this way!"

Antonio hurdled a tombstone and took off at a dead sprint, flying across the grounds of St. Marx. Sebastian jogged after him. Two minutes in, his eyes burned with sweat, his legs ached, and his lungs threatened to explode through his ear canals.

Eventually they reached a secluded, picnic-benched spot, and Antonio gave the sign to stop. Sebastian collapsed on the bench and panted, while his friend poked around for clues. A few minutes later, he pointed confidently to a bare patch of earth. "This is the place," he said, producing two shovels from his coat. "Let's do it."

Their shovels hit the dirt, and they began to dig. It was tough, brutal work. Beneath his gloves, Sebastian felt painful blisters forming. Antonio didn't seem to be in any discomfort whatsoever. The man was a machine. A top-hat-wearing, pocket-square-adjusting *machine*.

It took thirty minutes of nonstop effort to reach the casket. But finally Sebastian's shovel clinked against an old piece of stone, and after that it was quick work to pry off the decaying lid and bring the contents to the surface.

The contents.

A musty old skeleton, in other words.

It was brown with age, but wore surprisingly modern clothing. Jeans-and-tee-shirt modern. "This can't be him," Sebastian said.

"I'm tellin' ya, this is our guy. Now shush, so I can do some quick necromancin'."

Antonio lowered himself to the ground, sat cross-legged beside the skeleton, and mumbled a series of spells, prayers, and incantations. Sebastian didn't *know* they were spells, prayers, and incantations, of course—but judging by his friend's eerie tone of voice and the way his eyes rolled back in his head, he thought it was a pretty safe guess.

Suddenly there was movement. First a toe, then a kneecap. Then, as Sebastian watched, the entire skeleton rose to its feet. It turned its creaky head toward him ever-so-slowly. Its mouth opened, and it began chattering away in a language Sebastian couldn't understand. "What's he saying?" he whispered.

Antonio frowned. "He says he wants you to. . . *eat his farts*."

"That's Mozart, all right. C'mon, let's get outta here."

The skeleton crossed his arms and muttered something indistinct. Antonio looked up at Sebastian. "Not yet. He wants to know why you disturbed him."

Sebastian dropped to his knees. "It's like this, Mozart. I'm a composer. You know, like *you*. Anyway, I need your help. I wanna create something *amazing*. Something that changes the world."

Antonio relayed the message to Mozart, who hissed something in response. Antonio shrugged. "He says no."

"Look, dude," Sebastian said. "Just *one song*, all right? One puny, insignificant song, and I'll let you go. You can get back to your nice little dirt nap."

Before Mozart could answer, the beam of a flashlight struck his hollow, worm-filled eye socket. A voice shouted something in German, but Sebastian didn't wait for Antonio to interpret. He threw Mozart over his shoulder and ran. Antonio followed, and soon they had cleared the front gates.

Their getaway van was in sight, but the footsteps of the anonymous flashlight enthusiast were growing louder and louder. As he reached the vehicle, Sebastian could hear the echoes not ten feet away. "Shotgun," Mozart moaned, his undead fingers reaching for the passenger-side door. "Shotguuuunnnnnnn. . . "

"Don't think so, pal," Sebastian said, swatting Mozart's hand away and tossing him in the backseat.

"Got ya!" the guard screamed, his fingertips pinching the back of Sebastian's neck. Sebastian ducked out of his shirt and slid into the front seat, slamming the door before the man realized he was holding a bodiless shirt. Then tires were screeching, gravel was flying, and the van was spinning a wide arc and making its escape. Sebastian imagined police sirens and Austrian SWAT vans and helicopters screaming after them, but reality was much less dramatic. Reality was a single guard huffing and puffing down the road, shaking a sweaty shirt after them in fury.

Their van tiptoed through the night. Antonio took the scenic route, sticking to backroads and the occasional dark alley, and eventually they pulled up in front of their rented flat in eastern Vienna. They climbed the stairs, supporting Mozart between them like a drunken friend. Sebastian opened the door and pushed the skeleton inside, and the trio collapsed on the welcome mat.

"We did it," Sebastian said. "We actually *did it*, man."

Antonio shrugged. "Now what?"

"Let's make some music."

He turned to give Mozart a high-five, but the musician had moved to the window, where he stood at the curtain, running it through his fingers like he had never seen anything like it before. Sebastian walked over and threw his arm around him. "Yo Wolfie," he said, "let's quit messin' around and get to work, huh?"

He pointed past the kitchen and into the dining room, where an electronic keyboard had been set up. Mozart moved obediently to the piano bench. He sat down, cracked his knuckles, and looked expectantly at Sebastian.

"He needs details," Antonio said. "What do you want to say with this piece? What's the grand purpose?"

Sebastian rubbed his hands together. "It's gonna be great, man. What we're workin' on here is a soundtrack for a new video game. A first-person shooter. You know, *pew pew pew*! It's gonna be sick!"

After Mozart had listened to the interpretation, and Antonio had explained the meaning of video games and first-person shooters, and had further explained modern teenagers and Mountain Dew and basement boredom, Mozart dropped his forehead onto the keys and wept. It lasted two or three uncomfortable minutes, but finally he wiped the tears from his rotten eye-holes and whispered something in Antonio's ear.

"He says the cruelty of your request torments his very soul."

"Yeah, well, could you tell him to suck it up? I'm workin' on a deadline here."

Mozart stared at the keys for several moments. Sebastian hit record on his phone, placed it beside him on the bench, and stepped back to let him work in peace. After another brief crying session, he sighed and began to play.

It was magical.

The plastic keys sang wonderfully under Mozart's decaying hands. The song began softly, almost a lullaby, but gradually worked its way to a raucous, explosive, downright *religious* climax that kicked Beethoven's "Moonlight Sonata" in the teeth and gave Mussorgsky's "Night on Bald Mountain" a gas station swirlie.

"I've never been so moved," Antonio said. "I think I'm gonna cry."

"Wasn't bad," Sebastian agreed. "I mean, it's no Haydn, but it oughta do. Let's try another one. Gotta get my money's worth, don't I?"

Mozart turned on his bench and glared up at him. At least, his gaping nightmare sockets would have been glaring had there been any flesh on them.

"What are you doing?" Antonio asked.

"What do you mean?"

"One song, remember? That was the deal. One song and you give him his freedom."

Sebastian threw his head back and let out a Disney-villain cackle. "And you thought I was serious? This is only the beginning. You think I dug up the *best musician who ever lived* for *one* song? One teensy-weensy song? I don't think so. I'm sittin' on a *goldmine!*"

Antonio frowned and crossed his arms. "Ain't right, bro. Ain't right."

Sebastian ignored him and yanked Mozart up by his clavicle. "Welcome to the real world, Mozart! Now, back to work!"

Mozart slapped him so hard his ancient hand shattered into hundreds of dusty fragments. Sebastian reeled backwards, sneezed, and tripped. He landed on his back, and almost immediately Mozart was on top of him, his remaining hand clasped tight around his throat. Sebastian gurgled and threw wild punches, eventually making contact with Mozart's temple and knocking the maestro to the floor. He leapt to his feet and ran for the door, but Antonio beat him there and blocked his exit.

"You're not going anywhere until you give him his freedom."

"Outta my way!"

"You *promised.*"

"What is this—Girl Scouts? Lemme out, or I'll—"

His head jerked back before he could finish his sentence. He hit the ground with Mozart's ancient elbow digging into his kidney. He flailed around on the carpet, begging Antonio to tag in. But his friend stood unmoved. Then Mozart kneed him in the crotch and wrapped him in an unshakeable headlock.

"Fine!" Sebastian squeaked. "I'll give you your stinkin' freedom! Happy?"

Mozart returned to the keyboard. He unplugged it from the wall, carried it to the living room, raised it over his head, and brought it down on Sebastian's skull with a painful-sounding thud. He then turned his attention to Antonio, who stepped aside to let him pass.

A minute later, there was a terrible scream from the streets below. It was followed by the unmistakable sound of guts spilling onto the sidewalk. "You fool!" Sebastian shouted. "Do you know what you've done?"

"What?"

Another shriek from the street below.

"Didn't you ever watch *Frankenstein*?"

Antonio shook his head. "I don't believe in motion pictures."

"Of course you don't. But you can't just let the undead outta your sight like that, man!"

"Why not?"

"*Duh*. Because they'll go on a homicidal rampage! That's what they *always* do!"

"Oh."

Antonio helped him to his feet, waited for Sebastian to recover from his piano-induced dizziness, and together they raced down the steps. The squelching, splatting noises grew louder as they went, and as they reached the last step, Antonio gasped.

There weren't any dead bodies. The scene before them wasn't a gorefest. Instead, Mozart stood atop a parked car, waving a baton and directing a choir of. . .

The dead.

Skeletons lined the streets and sidewalks, singing an a capella hymn that brought tears. The tune was haunting, ethereal, and heart-stoppingly tragic.

"Not half bad for a bunch of dead dudes," Sebastian said. He pulled out his phone to record the new song, but a cold hand on his wrist stopped him. Antonio's eyes were angry.

"You're *not* recording this."

"Says who?"

Antonio snatched the phone out of Sebastian's hands and smashed it against the brick wall. He let it fall to the concrete steps and stomped it with his Fred Astaire shoes. Then he dusted off his hands and turned back to watch the performance.

"Kind of an overreaction, don't ya think?"

"Do yourself a favor, Keytari. Just *listen* for once. You might learn something."

Mozart's midnight chorus echoed up and down the cobblestone streets. It was beyond wonderful. It was Bach on acid, Vivaldi on 'shrooms, Tchaikovsky in Technicolor. It was a convent in a hurricane. Cathedral chants and wordless harmonies and silky arias wrapped their eardrums in angelic papier-mâché ecstasy.

Then the song was over, and Mozart and his undead bandmates evaporated, their bodies churning in silver, sighing coils before they disappeared in the fog.

"I get it now!" Sebastian said. "I *get it*. It's beautiful, Antonio! It's a masterpiece, a work of art, a—"

Antonio turned to smile at his friend. But something was wrong. Sebastian was on his knees, his body writhing, his mouth open in a silent scream. Then he began to disintegrate, his skin bubbling and steaming, until finally he was nothing more than a puddle of ooze on the sidewalk.

A moment later, the ooze began to gurgle and foam, and a much different man rose from the mess. His skin was pasty white, and a chalky wig hung lopsided on his head.

"Wolfgang," Antonio said. "Lovely to see you again."

"Eat my farts, Salieri," Mozart said. "A most insufferable young man, wasn't he?"

Antonio winced. "Quite insufferable."

"I must commend you on your mastery of the arcane arts. I had my doubts you would be able to restore me."

"But the young man, Wolfgang! I watched him waste away in agony! I watched his dying—"

"You bore me, Salieri. It was a necessary sacrifice. We both agreed on that."

"Yes, but—"

"Come, we have. . . *work*. . . to do."

Mock Me Amadeus

Antonio paused, remembering his friend's warning about Frankenstein and the inevitable homicidal rampages of the undead. What if Mozart had enlisted his help just so he could go on a murderous spree?

Impossible.

Then again. . .

Mozart frowned. "Are you coming, my friend? My requiem awaits."

Antonio laughed and embraced him. "Your *requiem*! Of course, Wolfgang! Of course!"

The two men climbed the stairs and re-entered the flat. Mozart picked up the keyboard, checked it for damages, and returned it to its stand. He plugged it in, took a deep breath, and ran his knuckles lovingly over the keys. A moment of hesitation, and he began.

Salieri watched in awe as the maestro's fingers danced a masterpiece.

About the Author

Justin Short is from Kansas City. His stories have appeared in places like *The Arcanist*, *Jerry Jazz Musician*, and Third Flatiron's *Galileo's Theme Park*. Visit his website at www.justin-short.com.

*****~~~~~*****

Toxic

by Eleftherios Keramidas

I knew of the deaths. The final pages of the victims' notebooks missing, torn away. Their brains wrecked, without any external trauma. No necromantic trick would recall their specters for questioning. Trying to peer back in time, to witness the events preceding their demise, proved not only just as fruitless, but also dangerous—the spirit realm around the corpses had grown hostile, choke-full with thorn bushes made of pure horror and hatred.

But a modicum of danger on the path to immortality could be expected, and I kept a few more tricks up my sleeve than all those wizards and witches who had failed with the deleterious grimoire.

I felt my way down to the basement store's entrance. Very little moonlight shone on the narrow steps, even less on the door. Barely enough to make out the large metal ring hanging from a maned head's jaws. The shadow of the lintel obscured the rest of the knocker's features, yet I guessed it wasn't a lion; a manticore, the mythical man-eater, seemed a much more fitting sign for the emporium of forbidden knowledge.

Soon after the third rap, I heard five locks turn successively and then as many latches slide. Hinges squeaked, the door opened a crack, pale light seeped out. Perched between a wrinkled, dark-skinned forehead and a hooked nose, a dark eye peered at me through the gap. It was the proprietor himself, the old Armenian. The man who had recently acquired the unique tome I sought.

He scrutinized me for a while, then unfastened the security chains and stepped aside. After I crossed the threshold, he took his time to secure the door again. I snapped up the chance to inspect the room. Most surfaces had sigils of protection inscribed on them. Bands made of the seven planetary metals reinforced the doorframe. The air was sweet with the smell of incense–and also bone-dry, as was necessary to preserve all those old volumes. I counted seventeen stacks of books, as tall as the ceiling allowed, spaced all too regularly on the circumference of a round rug. I surmised there was a magic circle hidden underneath.

A velvet curtain stretched from wall to wall in the back. Music came from somewhere beyond it, a dirge played on a psaltery.

The elderly man dragged his bad leg to the carpet's very center.

"Are you sure you want it?" he asked, his accent vaguely French. "It has done away with occultists far better known than you."

Doubtless, they had all been as well shielded against curses and spells as I could ever be. That's exactly why I suspected that a more mundane factor might also be involved: a toxin or virus, or maybe radiation. So, I left no avenue open for such a lethal agent to reach me. I was wearing a cap drawn as low as my ears. Gloves too. A thick scarf covered my neck, my mouth, and my nose. Ensorcelled obsidian-lens spectacles hid my eyes. For added protection against poison and disease, I had embroidered the Four Seals and the Three Symbols on every item of clothing touching my body.

So, I offered no answer to the old Armenian's attempt to dissuade me from obtaining the Nameless Book, I just snorted in derision. He shrugged.

I understood why he didn't care either way. Grimoires designed to store eldritch power as well as knowledge develop an aura that binds them with their owners in very specific ways. I know of one tome that cannot be given away or sold, only stolen. I know of another which can only be won through gambling. More than a few have a caretaker, a person they have made immortal and can always return to, no matter what.

Not that the Armenian was such a designated guardian. The Nameless Book would never abide one. The birth of its legend has no identifiable details and hasn't been tracked back to a specific time or source. The whole mystery—lack of known title and provenance, author, and synopsis—is the source of its might.

No one has ever tried to perform a ritual of binding to Name this grimoire and subjugate it. There hasn't even been anyone brave enough to give it a sobriquet for use in casual conversation. Manuscripts of power may be barely self-conscious, yet they possess potent will. Threatening the Nameless Book's autonomy even through a moniker would cause it to strike back. To strive for the complete annihilation of the offender, so as to subsume that person's story into its own and thus remain anonymous.

However, the Armenian's defenses had proven effective against temporary ownership of the Book. So, he surrendered it only when I paid a price he considered fair.

It was wrapped in violet silk, full of apotropaic symbols stitched in silver thread. The large metal clasps poking at my ribs as I carried it under my arm were the least of my worries; after I caressed it over the fabric—the cover was hard and creased, like bark—there was no way to stop repeating this movement over and over. I longed to riffle through the pages; everyone who has heard of the Book knows of its beautiful symmetry: it can be read left to right or vice versa, top to bottom or the opposite.

I became agitated, almost aroused. Only when I entered my home, my sanctum, did the feeling subside. The sense of total safety calmed me down. My walls, ceiling, and floor are all marked with protective polygons. I have even bound a small spirit to each piece of furniture, to keep other incorporeal entities out. My lab, the hub of my home and my work, while shielded in the same way, is also a sterile and mechanically automated environment.

Knowledge is freely available nowadays, especially through the Internet, the ubiquitous book. Even true occult lore can be discovered online, and this has helped the Art forge ahead. Yet only a few practitioners have come to realize how truly useful the leaps and bounds of this era's science can be. The slightest inexactness in a simple pentacle, an imperceptible discontinuity in its lines, results in death, insanity, or possession by otherworldly beings. I do not have to worry about such perils, though, since my magical diagrams are laser-cut. Any mistake while following an alchemical recipe may bring disaster. It's impossible for me to make such a mistake; I weigh materials with an analytical balance that is precise down to micrograms, then mix them with high-end medical equipment and apply my elixirs with industrial sprinklers—uniform pressure per square inch guaranteed.

There are far-UVC lamps all over my place, inactivating airborne bacteria, but in no way did I consider this treatment sufficient when I returned with the Book. I put the tome in the lab's airlock, then ran to the decontamination chamber, dropped my clothes in the incinerator, and proceeded to get rid of all biological, chemical, and radioactive agents I might have picked up, either in the basement bookstore or during my brief contact with the grimoire.

By the time I was purified, the rolling belt had moved the Book to the leaden box; its walls are lined with a plastic compound of my own design, incorporating twelve magical axioms in the macromolecules that comprise it. Inside the box, the Book was photographed by normal and by Kirlian cameras, subjected to several kinds of spectroscopy and checked for magnetic properties.

The resulting files were auto-saved to my computer's hard drive. I skimmed through them and set up a 3D model from X-ray scans of the mechanisms inside the grimoire's clasps. Others may have toiled for days or months to unlock them. I was done in less than half an hour. I programmed the robotic arms and then performed some rituals while they were pressing here and there on the Book's cover.

Finally, I took my vestments off, inscribed runes with pure henna on my chakras and wrote passages from the Forbidden Sutra on my face. Fully prepared, I sat before my desk and spent a moment trying to guess how the Book delivered its venom. Was it the ink? The edge of the pages? Rusty bands on its back?

All too many reasons not to touch the thing. I own the equipment to photograph text in rolled scrolls and closed tomes, page by page, layer by layer, telling each apart through the use of T-waves; it's the same technology applied on papyri charred by Vesuvius. So, I could even have skipped unlocking the clasps. But reading the Book was not my sole ambition. I wanted to crack its mystery and find out exactly how it murdered wizards and witches. If that proved impossible, I would settle for making it harmless.

In my studies, I have concluded that fame equals immortality. Legend is literally magic; it utilizes neither ceremony nor chant, it eschews sigil and potion, yet is as effective as any other form of the Art. Hercules and Gilgamesh, Marilyn Monroe and Elvis, Napoleon, all of them endure as more than stories; occasionally, they even awaken.

When the Armenian warned me that the Book had done away with occultists far better known than me, he mistook my lack of acclaim for lack of skill. The truth is I had never before sought to advertise my achievements. But were it to become known in certain circles that I had read the deadliest manuscript of power and furthermore broke it to my will, the legend of the Book would be incorporated in my own legend and become my ticket to life everlasting, my Philosopher's Stone.

Inside the leaden box, the robotic arms were already turning the pages. Each vellum surface was being vacuumed, sprayed with disinfectants, bombarded with radiation detrimental to all types of microorganism, and finally scanned. My Optical Character Recognition software was set to process the files as soon as it received them, equipped with all alphabets I could find in libraries across the world, plus a few familiar only to the initiated.

Looking directly at the Book's pages was out of the question, as a hex might have been scrawled in the margins or lurking in the illustrations. Even opening the grimoire using the robotic arms could have caused a demon or other hostile entity to appear. But that had been an eventuality I was well prepared for. My lab is fortified with several layers of containment circles.

From the very first moment the Book's cover was lifted, speakers around me were broadcasting exorcisms, entrapments and abjurations, in my own voice. By recording and mixing, you can redo any part, expel any error, achieve perfect rhythm and utterance of the words. Alas, sound alone carries little impact, unaccompanied by concentration. But the playback couldn't hurt, so I had turned it on.

Toxic

The scanning software issued a warning about empty files. I wasn't worried initially; blank pages at the beginning are part of the bookbinding process. However, thirty-four pages in a row without any text at all seemed unlikely. Then another thing, even more improbable, caught my eye. The size of every file, from the thirty-fifth scanned page on, was identical. I opened one, pretty certain I had botched the digitization.

The file's header informed me that no character on the page had been identified; I had to look at an image. It wasn't a photograph, just an approximation of ink outlines through a graphics editor, inserting yet another buffer between me and the Nameless Book.

I scrolled down. No spacing, no paragraphs, no punctuation. Just solid blocks of symbols neither curvilinear like Arabic nor angular like ancient Greek. There was a balance to them, adding. . . depth, if I may call it that. It felt like seeing beyond the liquid crystals of the screen. I opened a word processor and turned on the voice-to-text feature, so that I could keep some notes without switching between applications.

Back to the image, I stared at each character in turn. A flash of pain through my sinus made me squint. Then, I realized one ideogram had become highlighted in a way I can't describe precisely. It was as if it protruded from the page, reached my forehead and penetrated my skull, pushing part of my brain to a new configuration, one that allowed me to understand it. Depending on context, it meant "well" or "lair" or "tomb."

I scrolled up and down. Every time I located the same character, it stood apart and extended even deeper inside me. More ideograms came alive; I was learning them by revelation. I became fixated. I started making sense of whole sentences. The text was being filled out like a puzzle, one piece here, there another. It was a second-person narrative, the Book was addressing me. Only a handful of characters still eluded my grasp, threads in a torn curtain I would soon part to confront some primal truth.

A single drop of blood trickled slowly from my nose. I found myself unable to lift a hand to wipe it away. My mind was being rearranged like a Rubik's Cube, to fit the Book's contents. All other functions of my nervous system were being aborted as unnecessary. I was wheezing, my heartrate was dropping.

I decoded the text's secret. Me at its center—protagonist, narrator, and reader all at once. There was enough original information to intrigue, to lure in, but the rest had been drawn from my own psyche and memories, dressing the whole thing up. The Nameless Book is different for each owner. Personalized.

Through sheer effort, I managed to tear my gaze away for a moment and peeked at the size of the open file: zero. So, the ideograms were neither lighting up nor popping out of the text as I was learning them. They were actually vanishing, sublimated, migrating within me. It was all an illusion, I just thought I could still see them, because they were taking over whole regions of my mind. This is the way the Nameless Book kills. Each of its pages is a vessel, filled with a lethal dose of some toxic language.

I wonder.

Is this mortiferous grimoire an insidious ploy to destroy occultists who get too powerful or too ambitious? Or is it part of a scheme even subtler, grand and terrible, with the pages draining something indiscernible from the victim as they turn blank, until—after many centuries—a predesignated amount of this mysterious quality accumulates? If either of these theories hold any truth, then who has orchestrated the whole thing?

Maybe everything is much simpler. Maybe the Nameless Book is alive, hunting and feeding. Or it's just text, but meant for intellects vastly alien or superior to ours, the deaths of human readers being an unintended side effect.

Do the ideograms bear any meaning, or are they simple germs of the mind, serving no greater purpose in the universe than the cholera bacterium or the tuberculosis bacillus?

So many possibilities, so few clues. . .

Whatever the Book's true nature, will my scans vanish after I die? Or have I created a digital copy able to spread to every computer in the world? I underestimated all those who tried to read this grimoire before me. They all had the willpower to destroy their notes, as a precaution against further contagion. However, I can't even summon the strength to press a few keys and wipe the memory of every of my lab's devices. I am barely keeping myself from falling off the chair. And I read on, in the footsteps of Oedipus, the archetype of just not letting a mystery go.

Every other muscle in my body has gone numb, except those of my tongue. I guess the etchings on the ring that pierces it are just right for this situation. Anyway, I can still speak, and the word processor is turning whatever I say to text, the very text you are now reading.

Those whose lot is to keep the Art hidden from prosaic eyes shall eliminate all definite proof of my existence. I do not name their group here, lest they consider my narrative a threat and suppress it. No, this must not be done; I want this text to circulate freely.

A vocal command and it will be saved and uploaded to the Internet.

Without any evidence to back it up, most people will label it either a hoax or a work of fiction. But there are also the gullible and the seekers; they shall embrace it and repost it wherever they can. And my last two words shall be my name, my signature. Yes, I choose to become associated with the infectious grimoire, to open up a channel between us. I'm dying; I have nothing left to fear.

The more people talk about this story, the tighter my bond to the Book will get. I've told you enough to dispel—de-spell—some of its mystery, without exposing you to danger. Through this text, I am stealing some of the grimoire's thunder; even the initiated shall mention me once in a while, to specify the tome. Thus I have succeeded in labeling it; it's not entirely without Name anymore.

I will not attain immortality this way, however. I'm being annihilated. No fragment of my consciousness will be left behind to feed upon my legend. I didn't manage to appropriate the Book's power. Yet, through technology, I pare it down.

About the Author

Eleftherios Keramidas is a software analyst moonlighting as a spec-fic author. A Greek-language version of this story was included in "Applied Mythmechanics", a fundraising anthology for SFF.gr, the Greek speculative fiction forum. He is the author of a fantasy trilogy in Greek, entitled, "The Sons of Ash," and his short stories have been included in speculative fiction anthologies. In English, he appears in the Zombies Need Brains anthology, *Apocalyptic.*

*****~~~~~*****

The US Portal Service

by Brenda Kezar

"Guys! It happened again. Somebody broke in and ate my goddamn prime rib!" The screen door banged behind Charlie as he stepped out onto his front porch. Next door, Gerald and Pete stood beside Dan as he idled his new lawn tractor on his well-manicured lawn.

"What?" Dan scowled and turned off his tractor.

Charlie stomped down his steps and across the lawn, his face red and blotchy. "The prime rib I had in my fridge. It's gone."

"Are you sure you didn't eat it and just forgot? None of us are getting any younger," Pete laughed.

Gerald chuckled and held up his hands. "Don't look at me. Ever since my last cholesterol check, Lisa won't let me touch meat."

"Knock it off," Charlie scowled. "Like I told you before, it's the damn portal worker. He's been in my house again."

"Come on," Dan said. "Why would our portal worker be breaking into your house?"

"Don't they take a vow?" Gerald asked. "The US Portal Service Oath, or something like that?"

"Nah, you're thinking of the old-fashioned Postal Service." Pete snapped a mock Boy Scout salute. "'Neither rain, nor sleet, nor snow,' but they don't have to deal with any of that now that they've got delivery portals."

Charlie shook his head and started to turn away. "I've had enough. Before this goes any further, I'm going to file a complaint. I'll write to the Portalmaster General, or my congressman—"

"Don't you dare!" Gerald grabbed his arm. "Don't you remember how bad it used to be? All the porch pirates! I had to rent a locker and pick up my packages on the way home from work."

Gerald let go of Charlie's arm and dropped his voice to a near-whisper. "I hear they shut down portal delivery in places where they got too many complaints. Please don't make them shut down our neighborhood."

"I've got to do *something*." Charlie thought a moment, tapping one finger against his chin. "Dan, you still got those trail cams?"

"I've got two," Dan said. "Rain got inside the third and fried the electronics. Why?"

"Get one for me. I'm going to get proof."

As Dan climbed off the mower, Pete backed up out of his way, and Charlie noticed the goose egg in the middle of Pete's ever-growing bald spot.

"What the hell happened to you?" Charlie asked, as they followed Dan into the garage.

Pete grinned and gingerly rubbed the spot on the back of his head. "I was getting busy with my Tinder date. I never even heard the portal activate. Next thing I knew, my delivery from that internet shave club slammed me in the back of the head. I sure hope the mailman can't see us when those mail portals open, or he would've gotten an eyeful."

"Geez, they should get hazard pay if they have to watch you shaking your hairy ass," Gerald swiveled his hips and laughed.

"What's your portal generator doing in your bedroom?" Charlie asked.

Pete grinned sheepishly. "Who said it's in my bedroom?"

"There's an idea," Gerald shook his finger at Charlie. "Why don't you move your portal to the garage? Might solve your problem."

"Well, just be careful where you put it." Dan studied the garage shelf for a moment, then pulled a box down and set it on the floor. "We had ours near the dog's bed last election cycle. He almost got crushed under a wave of election junk mail one day. Now he runs like his tail is on fire every time he hears the portal engage."

They all laughed. "You should video it sometimes, put it on YouTube," Gerald suggested.

Dan took a trail cam out of the box and handed it to Charlie. "I'm just glad he's scared of it. One less thing for me to worry about. I don't want to have to start over, housebreaking a new dog."

"Yeah, my uncle's dog tried to jump through one." Gerald shuddered. "You don't want to know."

"That's a bunch of fear-mongering bullcrap." Pete shook his head. "They're afraid it will kill the travel industry if people can just portal from place to place."

"Right." Gerald snorted.

"Seriously. Think about how long the oil industry has been suppressing any engine that wasn't gas-fed technology." Pete looked around and then leaned in. "Wanna know what really worries me? Where did they get this technology? Have you ever thought about that? It's so far beyond anything we've developed before. It probably started in some secret Russian lab as a way to move spies around undetected. . . ."

"Man, you and your conspiracy theories." Gerald waved his hand dismissively. "They're going to be hauling you away in a damn white coat."

"And then you and Charlie can share a padded room," Dan snickered.

Charlie shook the trail cam at them defiantly. "You just wait. I'm going to get proof that sneaky bastard has been coming into my house. You'll see!"

. . .

The next day, Charlie arrived home from work and paused inside the garage to steady himself. This was it, vindication day. The proof could be waiting for him. He took several deep breaths and stepped inside.

At first glance, nothing looked out of place, but a faint, earthy smell hung in the air. Patchouli, maybe? Sandalwood? Definitely nothing he used. Someone had been in his house again. He broke into a grin.

Over on the coffee table, the new, unread National Geographic magazine he had left there that morning now sat at least two inches closer to the edge of the table. He leaned closer and held his breath. There, on the side of the magazine, was a brown smudge, and four brown crumbs lay on the table beside the magazine. His heart raced as he ran into the kitchen and threw open the refrigerator. The chocolate cake he'd had only one piece from now had a solid fourth of the cake gone. The stalker's appetite would be his downfall! Shaking with excitement, Charlie retrieved the trail camera card and went to his computer.

He had always assumed his ex-wife's cat did nothing but sleep all day, but the video proved him wrong. The cat apparently did a great deal of random wandering through the house, triggering the trail cam several times. At one point, the cat sat down in the middle of the carpet, threw one fluffy back leg high in the air, and began to lick its nether-regions.

He glanced over at the cat, currently swishing its tail on the other end of the sofa. "Why couldn't you take

218

care of that off-camera? Nobody wants to watch you lick your balls for an hour." Charlie growled and hit fast-forward.

He hated the cat, always had, but his ex-wife had insisted. Some couples have kids to try to salvage their relationship when it goes south. He and Jen had suffered with infertility, so when things began to go south, he bought her a cat. It was a big Persian that shed everywhere, and though his actual name was Royal Winchester Barclay the Third, Jen always referred to him as Mr. Fluffybottom. Charlie called him Fatass.

Jen hadn't been able to take the cat with her when she left him. His lawyer warned him not to get rid of the cat. It was her property, and the court would judge him harshly in the final divorce disposition if he disposed of her property. For now, he and the cat were stuck with each other. He guessed in a way, she had left them both, and they should be allies in their abandonment. But he hated cats.

After several minutes of fast forwarding, the portal began to glow. The video only had a side view because there was no good place to hide the camera looking directly into the portal. Not that it mattered, though, because Charlie was finally going to get proof someone was messing with him.

A second later, the video dissolved into snow.

"What the hell?" he barked. He fast-forwarded. More snow. Twenty minutes later, according to the timestamp, the picture came back. It showed his empty living room, portal deactivated, and mail in the basket. The only unusual thing was the cat sitting beside the mail basket, staring at the place where the portal had been, as if waiting for something. After a few seconds, the cat turned and left the frame. Charlie swore and fast-forwarded, but there was nothing else but Fatass occasionally wandering through the living room.

. . .

The next day, Charlie came home from work and hurried through the garage door. He was anxious to check the camera, but it would have to wait. He had been too eager to get home to bother to use the restroom before leaving work, and now he regretted it.

As he ran to the bathroom, his nose again tickled at the faint, patchouli-like odor in his house. He walked into the bathroom and froze. The seat was up. Sure, he and Jen had been split up a while, but not long enough for him to fall into bad habits yet.

He stepped closer. The water in the toilet was bright gold. *That*, he knew he didn't do. It had to be the portal worker.

His stomach soured at the thought. Not only was his portal worker sitting on his couch, reading his magazines, and eating his food, his portal worker was using his bathroom. Next thing you know, his portal worker would be sleeping in his bed and wearing his clothes, if he wasn't already.

Charlie used the guest bathroom, then returned and cleaned his own thoroughly. He checked the camera, but once again the video only showed Fatass passing back and forth through the living room, and only static from the moment the portal lit up until it shut down again.

Tomorrow was Saturday, though. Charlie was off on Saturday, and he would be ready and waiting when the portal opened.

. . .

According to the timestamp on the videos, the mail generally came between one and two o'clock. Charlie pulled one of the wooden dining room chairs in front of the portal generator at fifteen minutes to one. He opened a beer and sat in the chair to wait. Fifteen minutes passed, then twenty, then thirty, then forty-five. The beer had gone straight through him. His back was aching from sitting in the hard chair. He started to wonder if the mail was going to come at all. He checked his watch again and nearly jumped out of his skin when the portal suddenly buzzed into life.

The cat ran to the portal. Bathed in the blue glow from the portal, it mewed loudly, and then glared at Charlie with a look that clearly said, *why are you in my spot, human?* A piece of mail appeared and fell into the basket, and drew the cat's attention away from Charlie and back to the portal. There was a pause, and then another piece of mail fell.

Charlie leaned forward in the chair. He clasped his hands together to keep them from shaking. "Hey. You and I need to talk," he said into the portal.

As the next piece of mail slowly appeared, the cat reared up and batted at it. The mail dropped into the basket.

"Look. I don't know if you can hear me or not, but I know what you do when I'm not around."

Another piece of mail appeared, half in, half out of the portal. Charlie grabbed the protruding end. "Stop screwing with the cat and listen to me."

Charlie yanked the piece of mail with such force he wondered if it might pull the worker himself through the portal with it. The piece of mail came through the portal with no resistance against Charlie's momentous tug, and it caused his chair to rock backward and almost spill him out of it. The wobbling of the chair startled the cat, and it disappeared down the hallway.

Once Charlie caught his balance, he leapt out of the chair and squatted in front of the portal, peering into its mirror-like surface. The cat tentatively returned and began rubbing back and forth across his knees, as if to apologize for playing with the mail.

"Hey," he yelled into the portal. "Are you listening to me?" No mail popped through, but the portal didn't vanish, either. Was the portal worker listening?

"I don't know why you picked me, but I want it to stop. You hear me? If it doesn't stop, I'm going to contact the authorities!"

A single piece of junk mail popped through the portal and fell past Charlie's knees, into the basket.

"You hear me?" Charlie asked again.

Another piece of junk mail appeared and hung in the air, cut-in-half by the portal, and then became whole as it fell into the basket. Whoever was on the other side was toying with him.

"I'm not screwing around anymore." At that moment, perhaps sensing his agitation, the cat rubbed hard enough against Charlie's knees to knock him to the floor.

"Fucking cat," Charlie hissed. He grabbed the cat by the scruff of the neck, and without thinking, tossed the cat away from him. . . in the general direction of the portal.

The cat flew through the air as if in slow motion, toward the mirrored surface of the portal. Unlike the mail, the cat did not disappear bit-by-bit into the portal. Instead, the cat hit the portal and was transformed into eight pounds of pulverized blood and guts that flew back into Charlie's face as if he had thrown the cat into a fan made of knife blades.

The portal popped out of existence, and the few bits of Mr. Fluffybottom that had stuck to the surface of the portal dropped into the basket, on top of the mail, with a wet splat.

Charlie struggled to his feet. It looked like someone had left the lid off a blender. Red splatter covered every surface in a ten-foot fan-shape in front of the portal. He reached up and swiped a bit of Mr. Fluffybottom off his eyelashes. "Holy shit. Jen's never going to believe this."

. . .

Charlie woke with a cold on Sunday morning and dragged around the house all day. He felt worse on

Monday but still tried to go to work. He made it until lunch and then had to give up and go home.

In his driveway, he put the car in park and pressed the button on the garage clicker, but the door didn't lift. He tried it again and realized the remote wasn't even lighting up. "Great. What else can go wrong?" He tossed the clicker into the passenger seat.

He dragged himself out of the car and wobbled around to the side deck, fumbling for his key to the French doors. It had been so long since he had come into the house any way but the garage, he had almost forgotten what the key looked like. It took him a few minutes of struggle to find it.

As he lifted the key toward the door lock, he glanced through the glass. Inside, he could see his refrigerator door open, and someone in a gray trench coat leaning into his fridge. Rage boiled up in him.

His cold forgotten, he threw open the French door and roared, "GOT YOU!"

The person digging in his fridge straightened up. He—or it—was seven-feet tall, thin and gray-bodied, with spindly arms and legs, a bulbous head, and big, black, almond-shaped eyes. It looked straight off the cover of a Roswell tourist pamphlet.

"Jesus Christ." Charlie sagged. "That's not even funny. What if I'd had my gun on me? I could have shot you."

The person in the alien costume stood frozen.

"Funny, Dan. Take off the mask." Charlie took a step closer.

The person in the alien costume still didn't move.

"Joke's over, Pete. It's not funny anymore." Charlie stomped toward the person. As he drew closer, he could see it was a damn good costume, movie quality, even. Somebody had spent an awful lot of money on this practical joke.

223

Brain Games: Stories to Astonish

Brain Games: Stories to Astonish

"Seriously." Charlie reached out and closed his hand around the stick-thin arm. The too-thin arm. The warm, soft-skinned, not plastic-like at all, arm.

"Cinnamon," Charlie croaked. Now, closer and in the presence of his intruder, he recognized the earthy smell as closer to cinnamon. With growing dread, he looked up into the big black eyes as they stared back down at him. Ever so slowly, the big black eyes blinked.

A scream caught in Charlie's throat. He took a step backward, and as he did, his eyes fell on the lanyard around the thing's neck. The badge dangling from the lanyard read, in red and blue letters: US Portal Service. The creature snarled, revealing row after row of sharp little teeth. Charlie's last thought was that Pete couldn't have been more wrong about the portals being *Russian* technology.

About the Author

Brenda Kezar's stories have appeared in Third Flatiron's *Hidden Histories* and *A High Shrill Thump* anthologies, *Dark Moon Digest, Welcome to Miskatonic University* (Broken Eye Books), *Daily Science Fiction,* the "Tales to Terrify" podcast, and many others.

*****~~~~~*****

The Greatest Toymaker in the World

by Rebecca Fung

It's wrong to have favourites among your children. I don't have that problem. I can never choose.

Sometimes I've sincerely attempted to work out which of my gorgeous creations is most pleasing to me. Do I prefer the robots that swim or climb or fly; the toys with long limbs or that have small compact bodies, the unobtrusive ones or the ones that flash their many lights? The majestic huge structures, or the intricate, delicate little devices?

Too many, too many! They're all so precious to me. Every time I try to think it through, I fail.

"Next on your schedule is Hammond," said Siegfried, my assistant. I smiled. Hammond, the compact box-shaped puzzle robot, needed a new lighting display. I looked forward to working on him.

"We have half an hour. I'll update you on your most recent messages," said Siegfried. I liked this part of the day, listening to my fan mail.

"Thanks so much, how did you make the dinosaurs speak two hundred languages? You're a genius!"

"I love my new miniature Olympic Games—could you add gymnastics and hurdles, please please please."

"Best cooking game ever so much better than any other toymaker will get EVERY RECIPE you have I really like Japanese and Spanish food hint hint."

"Love the way the Rapunzel-doll's hair grows, does it grow forever—hope so—it would make me sooooo happy—and can it change colour? My sister says someone as clever as you would have made the hair colour changeable, can you write back and tell me which button I press?"

"My new remote-controlled teddy bear is so awesome. I don't know how you're going to top it this year—but I'm sure you'll think of something. I'm so looking forward to my next toy! I know you won't let me down."

I beamed as Siegfried read. He read me a selection each day. Every kid in the world (and quite a few adults) knew I was the best. The supreme. The almighty. There were some other weak toymakers who attempted to imitate me, with their poorly conceived and badly constructed pieces of work. They weren't even inventions, because they tried to copy everything that I'd done many years ago—a toy car or a doll here and there, with no ingenuity to it. Some of them could manage to make them move or talk but only with the most embarrassing creaky movements or squeaky voices. For a quality toy, I was the grand master of them all.

Siegfried organised my calendar, answered my mail, and put any necessary announcements out on social media. He knew me so well. I didn't want to be involved in such activities, but I did need someone to keep things running. It was a blessing to have someone I didn't have to explain every little thing to. I have programmed him to understand my every gesture, the raising of my eyebrow, each of my sighs. It's truly comforting to have Siegfried with me. Not only does he keep things going so smoothly. . . but, well, I don't have much company nowadays.

Once, long ago, of course, there was a wife. She waited patiently and made me cups of strong coffee as I worked, and looked very pretty in her housewifely dresses. I thought she was the most suitable forever companion. Then it began. That awful. . . human. . . part of her. The part where she started. . . feeling stuff and wanted me to as well.

"Coffee time!" Mrs Klaus trilled. "Oh, and you've got some mail!" She waved a handful of envelopes around.

"I'm working."

"You're always working. Oh, my Nicholas, I know that you love to invent new toys. And, of course, the children love you. These letters are so sweet and funny— 'Thank you for my choo choo train it goes fast please bring even faster one next year thanks'. But they're just toys. Choo choo trains. You can take a break for a while, it's not like someone will die."

"JUST TOYS!" I bellowed. "My work is the most important work in the world. I am an inventor, a magician. Any dream people have, I can create with a twirl of my hands, a bit of wood, glass, and metal and the right programming! My work gives meaning to life to millions of people worldwide. My name is whispered in every household. My rivals envy me."

"Of course, my dear," said Mrs Klaus. "What I meant was. . . your coffee is getting cold," she simpered.

"Later," I said. "I'm working on a new program for this coffee machine robot. You won't have to make me coffee, or bring it to me, anymore. Fully automated."

"Darling, I love to make your coffee. I know how you like it best. Isn't it best flavoured with my love for you?" She batted her eyelids.

"This new programming will go above and beyond anything any human can do," I muttered. "You'll be able to have coffee absolutely perfectly and won't even have to be interrupted with boring conversation! I'm a genius."

"Don't you love having your little coffee breaks with me? Couple time?" said my wife, pouting.

"Every second taken away from my work is a second one of my rivals could use to catch up with me. Not that they could get very far, because they aren't geniuses. But one must never get too complacent. Being the best and staying the best is what matters."

"Nicholas Klaus! You have your work; you also have a wife, you must remember. Look outside, dear. The first snowfall for the season! We could watch the snowflakes and drink our coffee. Wouldn't it be romantic?"

"I know I can get this code right. . . if I tweak the formula here. . . "

Burning coffee in one's lap is not conducive to producing more expert code. I learnt that lesson that night. Neither is going through a divorce. Fortunately, the former Mrs Klaus was not interested in my robots—my 'silly obsession with childish toys and experiments'. She wanted her jewellery and a nice big payout so she could buy a villa in France. Even though the settlement was amicable, it still took me unnecessarily away from my work.

Why, oh why, must women—in fact people in general—be so needy? It is an unattractive human trait that halts progress in this world. We could get so much more done if we didn't waste time staring at each other and needing to have "couple time" or "hang out and have a few beers together" for no other reason than to confirm that we are part of each other's communal network. A fact that one surely could establish early on, note in a data file, and stop this endless reassessment.

I could ruminate further, but I am not one to philosophise. Not when there's real work that needs doing.

Back to my inventions, I told myself. I finished inventing the automated coffee-server, whose gestures were gracious and never intruded on my work for a moment. Then I invented a multi-functional electronic diary-scheduler, several alarm clocks, and a mail-reader. As a bit of an indulgence, I worked on a mechanism inside a teddy bear so it would nod and agree with me, whatever I said. It became boring very quickly, so I programmed it to unpredictably disagree with me, for a bit of amusement and to prove that I could truly randomise my toys. I had disliked when Mrs Klaus interrupted and debated with me, but when this teddy bear did it, I loved it. It was proof of my skill. And of course, I could always dial his argumentative tone up or down as needed.

Then I built Siegfried. I've been building him ever since. He's my pride and joy among figurines. No doll moves so smoothly and unhesitatingly! If I ask him a question, you cannot hear the grinding of gears as he translates each question and searches for the correct toy-answer. No, his response flows magically. I have gifted him with the art of conversation, but more importantly, with non-conversation when appropriate.

And yet—oh joy—not that annoying prattle of humans. Every so often, I test Siegfried's ability to engage in meaningful conversation on an intellectual topic. Last night the topic was 'the representation of birds in modern art'. But most important is that Siegfried is programmed not to say anything at all when I'm working, or only to report for functional requirements. Ah, it's heaven!

Each day he reads my mail. I listen to the praise, and I take mental notes from the endless demands. Faster, stronger, higher, more lights, more sounds, more colour, more features, more combinations, more parts, can do more actions. Games with more variants. Dolls that are more realistic. Superhero figurines that are more and more unrealistic with all their powers—they can fly and be invisible and extra-strong and turn into animals and shoot laser-beams and bend metal bars with their minds—all at once.

Each day Siegfried brings me my list of next toys to work on. Hammond, then next it's Neptunia, the mermaid. Then Zappy, the rocket ship. And an army of vampire figurines need greater protection against the new strains of blood diseases that have mutated. A secretary doll must be programmed to learn the latest office software.

"So much to do and so little time," I say, but I'm enjoying myself. "If only these toys could fix themselves! What a perfect world that would be. Oh, Siegfried. I haven't seen Henrietta for a while. Make sure she's on my schedule."

Henrietta was one of my most treasured works, a doll that was not only beautiful with her head of golden curls and pearly skin but a programming marvel. I loved to work on her. Besides the thrill of finding Siegfried an even better update, Henrietta would rank as one of my work's greatest pleasures. She'd started off as an ordinary mechanical doll, but I had been the first to make her walk and talk. My programs were nothing like those primitive beasts my rivals attempted. I didn't give my creatures ten or twenty phrases they could blurt out in quick succession, such as "Hello Mama" and "How do you do?" and "I want a biscuit". No, Henrietta was far more sophisticated. I equipped her with a vocabulary that was larger than any little girl's she'd appeal to. She could construct original sentences and give long, engaging speeches. She could make jokes and throw temper tantrums, just like other little girls.

"I want lemon-and-sugar pancakes! Give them to me NOW!" she had screamed. "Not those nasty chocolate things, how crass! Lemon-and-sugar is the only kind of pancake I'll eat!"

She kicked her legs, thumped her fists on the ground, and even managed a very realistic set of tears. I fell in love with her, and most of all, with myself. Wasn't she gorgeous! All of my own hand!

"Henrietta hasn't been in touch for a long time," said Siegfried. "I don't think she'll be back."

"What do you mean?"

"Well, now that she's got her own home. . . " said Siegfried.

"You know that means nothing. I give all my toys away to little children," I said. "If I didn't, this whole workshop would explode at the sides. But you know they always come back for their improvements. Henrietta always did. The kids love it. I need to see her. There's always something that can be improved. She wanted a better singing voice. She wanted to learn to swim. And she had a little problem with her eye twitch. . . . I was going to fix that. I believe I can re-program something."

"All done," said Siegfried. He must have seen me gasp or something—I'm not sure what signal I gave out, but of course I betrayed my thoughts in some manner, and Siegfried read that. He's getting better and better.

"She taught herself to swim. She's improved her own singing. The eye twitch went away," said Siegfried. "She's a very intelligent and sophisticated doll. Of course, because you made her."

Siegfried was being very diplomatic. And of course, I should feel proud. Henrietta, my very own, smart girl, had taught herself to do all those amazing things and had fixed her own eye. It wasn't what I had expected. But then I kind of liked how randomly it had happened. It was like my disagreeing teddy bear. It was kind of cool that she had surprised me.

"You really are a genius," added Siegfried.

I'd been thinking the same thing. Although part of me had wanted to do all those things for her! When she had come in she had even called me 'Daddy'—wait, did she, last time? She had the time before, I was sure. Or maybe it was the time before that. When had she stopped? I can't quite remember. I wish she hadn't. I wanted to look after her again and let her sweet voice call me Daddy and curve into that beautiful smile.

"I'm happy for her," I said, but it sounded fake. "Bring in Hammond."

Hammond wheeled himself in and jumped up on my table.

"Good to see you, Hammond. Open wide!"

Hammond's puzzle box top clicked open. There were thousands of pieces with millions of combinations— I didn't like Hammond to be any ordinary puzzle. A new lighting display. I would make my Hammond sparkle. I tried to focus and push Henrietta from my mind. As I worked, I made mindless small talk.

"You're doing nicely with your set of wheels, Hammond."

"Thank you."

"Now, I'm programming you with several lighting variations. A neon combo, a standard rainbow, then an autumnal range and a sea range, and that knock 'em dead fireworks look. Oh yes. I can't remember when I gave you those wheels, but you use them superbly. You work the corners so well."

"Thank you," said Hammond. "I added the wheels myself. I wanted to do whatever I could to get to my scheduled appointments faster. The wheels weren't too tricky. It was very interesting, how they were done."

I stopped working on the light display. I didn't ask how he had obtained the wheels or figured out how. I examined him. They looked like my wheels. They were probably taken from my stash! But the way they were attached—the workmanship was excellent. I examined

232

them carefully. I didn't really want to admit this, but I could hardly tell any difference from my own work.

"Very good," I said. "You can close up your puzzle box now."

"Is it all finished already? You really are a genius!"

"The fireworks combination isn't complete. But you can make another appointment with Siegfried," I said. I just wasn't in the mood.

"Yes, thank you," said Hammond, flashing his lights and wheeling himself out. He flashed each combination over and over and began to hum. "Very interesting, how this is done," he mumbled. I realised I wouldn't see Hammond again.

This was strange. Naturally I was very happy for Hammond. Wasn't I? He was so happy with his wheels, and he'd done such a good job. And I'd done such a good job of him. I hadn't realised what a good job of him I'd done. My amazing ability was fantastic beyond even my own realisation. I was very proud. Proud of him, proud of Henrietta. I felt a tremor inside me. Feeling so proud had a hollow, empty feel to it.

I needed a few days off. The first few days off I'd had in my entire career. I can't even remember telling Siegfried, but a raised eyebrow or a twitch of the nose and he probably figured it all out. He was getting amazingly good at reading my body language. He didn't comment or question it. I didn't have to tell him—I knew he'd handle my schedule till I got back. But I needed breathing space.

. . .

"Siegfried!" I called out when I returned. "Who's next on my list?"

I rubbed my hands. A few days off had been enough; I really needed to see my toys again.

My voice echoed around the room. Where was Siegfried? It couldn't be his day off; I hadn't programmed him to have any days off.

233

I walked over to my scheduler. Usually I never glanced at it, because Siegfried maintained everything so well for me. It was blank, apart from a video file labelled "Farewell." My fingers twitched. They wanted to work, they wanted to be tweaking toys and making them better and better! But since they had nothing else to do, my finger pressed "PLAY."

"Goodbye, Mr Klaus. I've been planning my journey for a while; I thought it was right to make sure the list was cleared before I left, though. I know you didn't program me to think that, but I've been developing my own strong ethical framework for a while now. The rest of the toys are very able to look after and to continue maintaining themselves—you've been fundamental in giving themselves these rich lives. I'd like to say they'll never forget you, but I can't guarantee that; you never know what direction they'll grow in. But that's what you wanted, wasn't it—the unpredictability of the machine's autonomy? Congratulations! I assume those are tears of joy? Farewell."

I've done it, I thought, I'm the greatest toymaker in the world. No one else has made toys that don't ever need updating or fixing. No other toymaker could make a toy that could make its own decisions. All I ever wanted was to be the best. I said it over and over as my fidgeting fingers kept pressing PLAY. I listened to the recording over and over to hear the comforting tone of Siegfried's voice. I could feel something moist on my face. Joy tasted very salty.

About the Author

Australian writer Rebecca Fung has published stories in *Midnight Echo, Trysts of Fate, Voluted Tales*, and *Eclecticism* magazines and is a regular contributor to the "Demonic Visions" anthology series. Her story, "A Little Peace" was selected in 2016 to be published in *Midnight Echo's* "best of" issue, *Dead of Night.* She's also been published in many anthologies, including *Witches, Stitches and Bitches*; *Potatoes*; *Her Dark Voice; Daylight Dims 2; Between the Cracks;* and *Bloodlines.* Her children's book is Princess Hayley's Comet. Listen to her work on podcast on chillingtalesfordarknights.com

*****~~~~~*****

Grins and Gurgles

To All the Creatures I've Hid From Ethics Committees

by Aidan Doyle

I knew my plans would never be approved, so I created you in secret. My colleagues thought my work had stalled, but I was busy making the world's saviors. When I was ready, I announced your existence. I expected the world to be grateful, but instead they mocked us.

Recyclo, you are not a man-eating blob. You are the ultimate recycling receptacle. The future of a sustainable economy lies in your tendrils.

Winston, you are one of my greatest accomplishments. Half man, half WiFi. You bring the world to every conversation. People love you now, but humans can be so fickle. Will they love you as much

237

when they find a stronger and quicker version? You need to be able to distinguish between those who love you for who you are and those who want to use you to illegally download movies.

Bessie, my beloved fireproof cow, I wept when I saw those other firefighters laugh at you. "A cow will never learn how to use a high-pressure fire hose," they mocked. Then you extinguished that apartment building inferno by spraying fire retardant from your teats. You saved dozens of lives.

When I first joined the university, I proposed transforming the city's shores—solar-powered jetties, a mermaid-staffed desalination plant, and a bamboo coral fusion sea wall. No one appreciated that my coastal development plan was pier reviewed.

Instead, I went to work on solving the mystery of what was happening to the bees. That's where you come in, Queebee. The world's greatest bee detective. Your investigation into colony collapse disorder has already revealed insights with profound implications for how human society functions. We all need to care for each other.

Apart from ethics committees and lack of funding, the biggest problem holding back scientific innovation is bureaucracy. The pointless paperwork, the oh-so-tedious faculty meetings that never end. I don't like to play favorites, and I love all my children equally, but when the Nobel Committee realize their grave error and reply to my emails, they'll inevitably ask me what I'm most proud of and I'll answer Timezip. Half woman, half time compression algorithm. When you are present Timezip, we can get up to ten times as much done. A four-hour faculty meeting finishes in under half an hour.

My children, you have done so much for society and I know you are angry at how the world has treated you. Some fear you, and accuse me of wanting to take over the world. I have no plans for world domination. I've studied the literature and am aware of the failure rate for such schemes.

One of my grad school colleagues was always ranting about how inferior minds were as inconsequential as ants. I prefer to look upon the rest of humanity as akin to puppies. Sometimes they make a mess that needs cleaning up. It can be tiring to have them around, but ultimately they bring joy and happiness.

Most so-called evil geniuses fail to recognize the most important precepts of human psychology. World domination is not the surest path to happiness. All of the scientific literature says that keeping a gratitude journal and giving to others is more likely to make you happy.

Every day I write something about each of you that I'm grateful for. You've brought such joy into my life. I want the same for you, my children. Instead of destroying humanity, I ask that you to do something kind for someone every day. This will make you happier than seeking revenge on those who laughed at you. Like any good parent, I wish happiness for my children. Go forth my brave wonders, and be kind.

About the Author

Aidan Doyle is an Australian writer whose stories have been published in *Lightspeed, Strange Horizons*, and *Fireside.*

*****~~~~~*****

DIY Your Pillow!

by Steve Zisson

Infomercial Script for DIY Your Pillow!

Fade in:
Music theme comes up loud, generic punk rock.
Music fades to SPOKESPERSON sleeping blissfully with a Your Pillow!
S awakens, leaping from the bed like a punk lead singer crashing into the pit.
S is dressed in a mix of punk rock fashion, tinged with steampunk, cyberpunk.
S gestures wildly like Iggy Pop. They grab the pillow off the bed, cradling it.
They hold a Your Pillow! over their head as if they're going to smash a guitar on the stage like Paul Simonon.

S: This is my Your Pillow! No, not that guy's My Pillow. Screw him. I'm going to tell you how you can fight back against his fascist capitalist crap. I'm gonna show you how to make your own Your Pillow! This is revolution. It'll be exciting, so stick with us the next few minutes.

S unzips the pillow cover, pulling out little foam pieces.

S: All he did to make His pillow was cut up some foam, shove it back in, and spend millions advertising His pillow to jam it down the public's throat.

S puts the stuffing back in the pillow, returning it to the bed before sitting down.

S: You won't believe how easy it is! Take a pillow and cut up the foam inside into random pieces. You've got a Your Pillow!

S (*presses their head into it*): My Your Pillow! changed my life. A few years ago I hurt my neck during a show banging around the pit. Now I can go all night again.

Close-up of S showing great neck flexibility.

S: Don't take my word. Please meet another success story, JANIE JONES, who's feeling great about their life after making a Your Pillow! She's sleeping better than ever and bringing down the capitalist system too. Doesn't get any better than that. Come on out here, JANIE!

J (*hugging a pillow*): I gotta tell you how I made my Your Pillow!

S (*rubbing hands together, anticipating*): Tell us more!

DIY Your Pillow!

J (*taking crumpled paper out of a pillow*): All I did was scrounge some newspaper—

S (*concerned*): Bet it was hard to find newsprint.

J: Sure was. I did a lot of dumpster diving and even sacrificed some old zines. The zines give my Your Pillow! some shape, which I just love.

S: Using zines for filling must be so meaningful to you.

J: I sleep so soundly now because of just-the-right firmness and attitude inside. Before DIY-ing the shit out of this pillow, I was lucky to get three hours of sleep a night. I was so tired and cranky during the day. Now my friends are surprised at how alive I look!

S: Sleep is so important! Did you put anything else in there to make it Your Pillow?

J: Sure did!

J (*exposing a small clock*): I found this steampunk clock at a little shop, reverse engineered it, and sewed it into the pillow. Tick-tocking in my ear is soothing. I get to sleep faster and stay asleep.

S (*skeptical*): Wouldn't you wake up if you rolled onto hard metal?

J: Thought of that, so I mixed up an alloy. Alchemist-like. When the clock senses my head about to touch it, it goes all soft but keeps on ticking!

S: Ingenious! Magical! Thank you for telling us your story, JANIE. Inspirational! We just love Your Pillow! You made it yours!

J exits with their Your Pillow! raised above their head in triumph.

S: Time to wrap up. We've shown you everything you need to make Your Pillow! Don't rely on that My Pillow guy.

S (*glaring*): Here's our call to action. Don't send us money for pillows. Make a Your Pillow! DIY! Post-capitalism!

A final call-to-action scrolls on the screen: Please make a donation to our nonprofit that funds direct action at smotherthestatewithyourpillow.org.

About the Author

Steve Zisson is a biotech journalist who for many years was editorial director of a Boston-based clinical trials publishing company and senior editor at a biotech news outlet. His speculative fiction has appeared in or is slated to be published in *Daily Science Fiction, Nature's Future,* and *Selene Quarterly*, among other places. He edited a science fiction and fantasy anthology, *A Punk Rock Future*, published in 2019. Born in Salem, Massachusetts, he now lives in a nearby town.

*****~~~~~*****

The Best Bra for the Boobs

by Lauren Lang

I always wanted to go to outer space, though I should have been pickier about how I got here. I could have purchased a first-class ticket. Granted, that would have taken a lifetime, but at least I would have seen the next frontier with my clothes on.

The red lacy halter bra I'll be in for the next four hours chafes my skin, itching under my armpits. I've had it on for less than ten minutes, and I already want to rip it off and let the girls float free. The cups only cover half my chest, the deep V-neck leaving plenty of skin exposed. The tight strap around my neck keeps shoving my cleavage up toward my face. It's like looking down into the Grand Canyon, I'm so squished.

It's still better than the last get-up I was in. I kept spilling out of the strapless black satin demi push-up I was scheduled to wear before this. There's nothing worse than

245

trying to shove your tits out of your eyes so you can appreciate the view.

It's a sparkling carpet of stars, when I can catch a glimpse between the floating mass of satellites surrounding the planet. It's harder to see space out here than it is to find a bra that fits, and as every woman on Earth knows, that's saying something.

At least they're keeping it warm on the ship. I guess if you're going to have a floating barge full of half-naked ladies, you want to keep them comfortable. God only knows the intimates industry can afford it. They're worth over five-hundred billion a year, with an eye on expanding their market share to the Moon. What happens to boobs in space? That's what we're all here to find out. Product testers, each and every one of us a different size, shape, and color, are out here looking for ways to make a spacesuit sexy.

The photographer should be by soon. He needs images of me lounging on my back, hands carelessly tussling my long brown hair like I'm sunbathing on some exotic beach instead of floating weightlessly in this claustrophobic cabin. They haven't figured out how to market to the cosmopolitan woman of the cosmos. Maybe that's because she doesn't exist yet. If the marketing men have their way, she will before the first female foot ever steps on the surface.

At least they haven't handed me a cone bra yet, though, from the tall stack they gave me, I'll be trying every other style. My tiny cabin is littered with the stuff of an underwear model's dreams; a corset bra floats past the small porthole, a bandeau hits the bunk, and the bralette has become mixed up with the rest of my clothing. I'm *really* looking forward to untangling the straps of that last one from the arms of my shirt and slipping the soft cups over my irritated mammaries. It's the only comfortable-looking piece here, but then I'm convinced nothing could itch more than the brand-new, starchy, unwashed, lacy torture device I have three more hours in. It's driving me mad.

I think pasties are going to be the preferred undergarments of the spacefaring generation. We can all glue rhinestones to our nipples for that *extra* sparkle. We'll seduce our boyfriends while glittering like the stars themselves. We'll have ethereal areolas attached to boobs that never sag. We'll sashay across the surface of the Moon with long, graceful strides, the lack of gravity allowing even the tiniest titties to bounce in ways previously unimaginable.

There will be no place for plastic surgeons on that barren rock. No more facelifts or breast augmentations, only the occasional butt lift for the girl who didn't get enough of a boost from blasting her ass into space. Once we start creating Moon colonies, those girls will be way past my current low Earth orbit, but it doesn't mean their self-esteem will rise with the rocket. There will always be women who feel the need to be propped up by padding.

Two more torturous hours. I find it almost impossible to believe that a woman invented this contraption. Damn you, Caresse Crosby. I could have been in a corset. Now that's a sexy way to get a monobossom. I would have been far too covered up for the pictures, though.

I came up here hoping I could help women flounce forward, but that expectation is falling faster than the landing craft I'll be climbing aboard at the end of the week. Each time that shutter snaps, I can feel a little bit of my soul leeching out into the void, and I don't mean the one outside these bulkheads. I shiver with the cold realization that micrometeoroids and lunar dust might not be the only dangers women will face. We don't have the right tools to navigate the topography for a variety of reasons.

One more hour to go. There's a knock on the door, and I hit the button to let the photographer inside. He twists and turns me, looking for my best angle. I'm less friendly now that I understand what his is. I give him a smile, just like he asks, grimacing behind clenched teeth. He tells me to put my hand to my face, stroking my jaw with the backs of my fingers. My phalanges feel foreign, like I'm just a mannequin who can move. He takes what he needs and actually has the courtesy to leave, unlike some men. However, the encounter leaves me feeling similarly empty.

I stare out the window, watching endless space junk floating by. A bra bumps into my naked stomach, and I look down at the satin cups. It's all pretty garbage.

About the Author

Third Flatiron welcomes Lauren Lang, a new writer from Denver, Colorado. She is a former broadcast journalist and current freelance photographer and videographer. In her spare time, she writes, crochets hats for stuffed animals, gardens with the intent of taking pictures of the flowers should they live, and terrorizes residents while running through area parks with her camera screaming, "Birds!"

*****~~~~~*****

Credits and Acknowledgments

Cover: Keely Rew

"Editor's Note" - Shifted chessboard (or Münsterberg illusion). Example of a geometrical-optical illusion. Commons.wikimedia.org. Author:Laszlo Nemeth
"The Best Bra for the Boobs" – Wikimedia Commons file: Lady's corset, 1882 *Harper's Bazaar*

All other images: royalty-free stock art

*****~~~~~*****

Discover other titles by Third Flatiron:

(1) Over the Brink: Tales of Environmental Disaster
(2) A High Shrill Thump: War Stories
(3) Origins: Colliding Causalities
(4) Universe Horribilis
(5) Playing with Fire
(6) Lost Worlds, Retraced
(7) Redshifted: Martian Stories
(8) Astronomical Odds
(9) Master Minds
(10) Abbreviated Epics
(11) The Time It Happened
(12) Only Disconnect
(13) Ain't Superstitious
(14) Third Flatiron's Best of 2015
(15) It's Come to Our Attention
(16) Hyperpowers
(17) Keystone Chronicles
(18) Principia Ponderosa
(19) Cat's Breakfast: Kurt Vonnegut Tribute

Brain Games: Stories to Astonish

THIRD FLATIRON
www.thirdflatiron.com